DAVID COPPERFIELD

DAVID COPPERFIELD

Charles Dickens

Bloomsbury Books
London

This edition published 1994 by Bloomsbury Books, an imprint
of The Godfrey Cave Group, 42 Bloomsbury Street, London,
WC1B 3QJ.

ISBN 1 85471 253 5

Printed and bound by Firmin-Didot (France),
Group Herissey. No d'impression : 27614.

Contents

1

His Happy Childhood

David Copperfield never knew his father, for he died before David was born; but his young, beautiful mother, with her pretty hair, and soft, shining eyes, David never forgot.

When he looked back into the hazy days of his babyhood, she was the first person he remembered— his mother and Peggotty.

Peggotty's eyes were black, and her cheeks and arms so red, that David wondered that the birds did not peck her in preference to apples.

On the bright, windy March afternoon of the day that David was born, Mrs Copperfield was sitting by the parlour fire, when, lifting her eyes to the window opposite, she saw a strange lady coming up the garden.

Though she had never seen her before, the young widow felt positive that it was Miss Betsey Trotwood, her dead husband's aunt, of whom he had often spoken Her nephew had been a favourite of Miss Betsey's, but she was very angry with him for having married such a young, girlish wife. "A wax doll," Miss Betsey called her, though she had never set eyes on her till this present afternoon.

Instead of ringing the bell like any other visitor, she came and looked in at the window, pressing the end of her nose so close to the glass that it became quite flat and white with the pressure; and seeing the young girlish figure in widow's weeds, she beckoned to Mrs Copperfield to come and open the door

"Mrs David Copperfield, I think," said Miss Betsey, looking her up and down.

"Yes," said Mrs Copperfield faintly

"Miss Trotwood," said the visitor. "You have heard of her, I dare say."

Mrs Copperfield said she had.

"Now you see her," said Miss Betsey, following her hostess into the parlour.

Miss Betsey looked so formidable, and stared so hard, that poor Mrs Copperfield began to cry.

"Oh, tut, tut, tut," said Miss Betsey. "Don't do that! Come, come! Take off your cap, child, and let me see you."

Mrs Copperfield was too much afraid to refuse, so she took off her widow's cap, with such nervous hands that her hair, which was very beautiful, fell about her face.

"Why, bless my heart!" cried Miss Betsey, "you are a very baby!"

Poor Mrs Copperfield hung her head as if it were her fault, poor thing, that she looked so young; and while she sobbed and murmured that she was afraid she was but a childish widow, and would be but a childish mother if she lived, she fancied she felt Miss

Betsey softly touch her hair; but when she looked up, the visitor was sitting with her feet on the fender, and her hands folded on her knee, frowning into the fire.

"Have some tea," said Miss Betsey, seeing that the hostess looked faint; "what do you call your servant?"

"Peggotty!" said Mrs Copperfield.

"Peggotty!" repeated Miss Betsey indignantly. "Do you mean to say that any human being has gone into a Christian church, and got herself named Peggotty?"

"It's her surname," said Mrs Copperfield faintly. "Mr Copperfield called her by it, because her Christian name was the same as mine."

"Here! Peggotty!" cried Miss Betsey, opening the parlour door. "Tea. Your mistress is a little unwell. Don't dawdle."

Peggotty was coming along the passage with a candle, and stood amazed at the strange voice bawling out orders as if it belonged to the head of the house. Miss Betsey then shut the door again, and sat down as before, with her feet on the fender.

"And was David good to you, child?" asked Miss Betsey, after a short silence. "Were you comfortable together?"

"We were very happy," was the answer. "Mr Copperfield was only too good to me."

Peggotty came in by and by with candles and the tea, and seeing how ill her young mistress looked, she conducted her to her room, sent for the doctor, and left the strange visitor sitting by herself in the parlour.

David was born that evening; and by and by, Mr Chillip, the doctor, went into the parlour to speak to the strange guest. She had taken her bonnet off and had tied it, by the strings, over her left arm.

"How is she?" asked Miss Betsey abruptly, staring at the doctor, who was a very little man, in such a stern way that it made him nervous.

"Well, ma'am, she will soon be quite comfortable, I hope," returned Mr Chillip mildly, "quite as comfortable as we can expect a young mother to be. There cannot be any objection to your seeing her presently, ma'am. It may do her good."

"And *she*. How is *she*?" said Miss Betsey sharply.

Mr Chillip laid his head a little on one side, and looked at Miss Trotwood like an amiable bird.

"The baby," said Miss Betsey. "How is *she*?"

"Ma'am," returned Mr Chillip, "I apprehended you had known. It's a boy"

Miss Trotwood said never a word, but took her bonnet by the strings, in the manner of a sling, aimed a blow at Mr Chillip's head with it, put it on bent, walked out, and never came back. She was so disappointed that the baby was a boy.

Oh! those were beautiful days, the first years of David's childhood. And they were happy and merry always—he and the young, pretty mother, and faithful Peggotty.

Peggotty's kitchen opened out into a back yard; with a pigeon-house on a pole in the centre, without any pigeons in it, and a great dog-kennel in a corner, without any dog, and a number of hens and a cock that got upon a post to crow.

And there was a garden where he played, where ripe fruit clustered on the trees in the warm summertime; and at the bottom of the garden there were tall elm trees bending to one another in the breeze like giants whispering secrets, with ragged rooks' nests hanging on the topmost branches, that the birds had deserted long ago.

In the wintertime he played about the parlour, and learned his little lessons at his mother's knee, and danced with her in the firelight when the lessons were all done—a beautiful, happy time!

Peggotty and he were sitting one night by the parlour fire alone, for Mrs Copperfield had gone out to a neighbour's to spend the evening, and as a great treat David was to sit up until his mother came home. He had been reading about crocodiles, but was tired now, and very sleepy, though he would not have owned that for the world, of course.

"Peggotty," said he suddenly, "were you ever married?"

"Lawk, Master Davy," replied Peggotty. "What's put marriage into your head?"

"But *were* you ever married, Peggotty? You are a very handsome woman, an't you?"

"Me handsome, Davy Lawk, no, my dear! But what put marriage into your head?"

"I don't know! You mustn't marry more than one person at a time, may you, Peggotty?"

"Certainly not," said Peggotty.

"But if you marry a person, and the person dies, why then, you may marry another person, mayn't you, Peggotty?"

"You may," said Peggotty, "if you chose." And she looked curiously at David.

"You an't cross, I suppose, Peggotty, are you!" said David; because he really thought she was; for she had spoken rather shortly.

For answer, Peggotty laid aside the stocking she was knitting, and opening her arms wide, took the curly head within them, and gave it a good squeeze.

"Now let me hear some more about the Crorkindills," said Peggotty, "for I an't heard half enough." She looked very much moved, and David wondered why she looked so queer; but he went on reading again until the garden bell rang.

They went out to the door together, and there was David's mother looking unusually pretty, and with her a gentleman with beautifully black hair and whiskers, who had walked home with them from church last Sunday. Mrs Copperfield stooped down to take David in her arms and kiss him, and the gentleman said that he was a more highly privileged little fellow than a monarch.

"What does that mean?" asked David over her shoulder.

The gentleman only patted his head; but David did not

like him, somehow, and tried to put away his hand.

"O Davy!" remonstrated Mrs Copperfield.

"Dear boy!" said the gentleman. "I cannot wonder at his devotion."

A beautiful blush stole into Mrs Copperfield's face. She gently chided David for being rude; but pressed him close to her as she thanked her companion for having seen her home.

"Let us say 'good night,' my fine boy," said the gentleman, when he had bent his head over the mother's little hand.

"Good night," said David.

"Come! Let us be the best of friends in the world," said he, laughing. "Shake hands!"

David's right hand was in his mother's left, so he gave him the other.

"Why, that's the wrong hand, Davy," laughed the gentleman.

Mrs Copperfield drew his right hand forward; but David didn't like him, and would not give it, but persisted in offering the left. But the gentleman shook it heartily, and called him a brave fellow, and went away: and as he went he turned round in the garden, and gave them a last look out of his deep black eyes, before the door was shut.

Peggotty, who had not said a word, bolted and locked the door, and they all went into the parlour.

"Hope you've had a pleasant evening, ma'am," said Peggotty, standing as stiff as a barrel in the middle of the room, with a candlestick in her hand.

Mrs Copperfield answered cheerfully that she had had a very pleasant evening.

"A stranger or so makes an agreeable change," suggested Peggotty.

"A very agreeable change indeed," returned Mrs Copperfield.

David was half asleep; but he had an uncomfortable feeling that Peggotty was finding fault with his mother, and that his mother was trying to excuse herself, and was crying; and then Peggotty burst out crying herself, and David woke up and cried too, and they all cried together.

But the Sunday after that the gentleman walked home with them from church again, and David knew that Peggotty didn't like him any more than he did; but that didn't prevent Mr Murdstone from walking home with them again. And his mother wore in turn all the prettiest dresses she had in her drawers, and went to visit at that neighbour's very, very often.

One autumn morning, when David was about eight years old and was with his mother in the front garden, Mr Murdstone came by on horseback, and, reining up his horse, said he was going to Lowestoft to see some friends who were there with a yacht, and proposed to take David on the saddle before him, if he would like a ride.

The air was so clear and pleasant, and the horse seemed to like the idea of a ride so much himself, as he stood snorting and pawing at the garden gate, that David had a great desire to go. So he was sent upstairs to Peggotty to be made spruce; and in the meantime Mr Murdstone dismounted, and with his horse's bridle drawn over his arm, walked slowly up and down on the outer side of the sweetbriar fence, while Mrs Copperfield walked on the inner to keep him company.

Peggotty and he peeped at them from his little window, and Peggotty, somehow, was very cross, and brushed David's hair the wrong way, very hard.

But David was ready by and by, and they were soon off trotting along on the green turf by the side of the road. Mr Murdstone held him quite easily with one arm, and David felt a fascination in turning round to look up into his face; and though he could not make up his mind to like him any better, he thought he was a very handsome man.

They went to an hotel by the sea, where two gentlemen were smoking cigars in a room by themselves.

"Hulloa, Murdstone!" they cried, "we thought you were dead."

"Not yet," said Mr Murdstone.

"And who's this shaver?" said one of the gentlemen, taking hold of David.

"That's Davy," returned Mr Murdstone.

"Davy who?" said the gentleman. "Jones?"

"Copperfield," said Mr Murdstone.

"What! Bewitching Mrs Copperfield's incumbrance? The pretty little widow?"

"Take care, if you please," said Mr Murdstone; "somebody's sharp."

They walked about on the cliff after that, and sat on the grass, and looked out of a telescope, and then came back to the hotel to an early dinner; and then they went on the yacht.

There was a very nice man on board with a very large head of red hair, and a very small shiny hat upon it, who had got a cross-barred shirt or waistcoat on with "Skylark" in capital letters across the chest. David thought it was his name; and as he lived on board ship and hadn't a street door to put his name on, he put it there instead; but when he called him Mr Skylark, he said it meant the yacht.

They went home early in the evening, and Mrs Copperfield and Mr Murdstone had another stroll by the fence while David was sent in to get his tea; and when Mr Murdstone was gone, David's mother asked him what he had done all day.

And David told her everything, not forgetting to mention how one of the gentlemen at the hotel had called her "Bewitching Mrs Copperfield," and "The pretty little widow," which Mrs Copperfield said was nonsense, though she laughed too, and looked a little pleased.

"David, dear," she hesitated.

"Well, Ma."

"Don't tell Peggotty; she might be angry with them. I would rather Peggotty didn't know."

And David promised, of course.

2

His Visit to Yarmouth

"Master Davy," said Peggotty one evening, about two months after his ride with Mr Murdstone—they were sitting together, as Mrs Copperfield was spending the evening out—"Master Davy, how should you like to go along with me and spend a fortnight at my brother's at Yarmouth? Wouldn't that be a treat?"

"Is your brother an agreeable man, Peggotty?" asked David.

"Oh, what an agreeable man he is!" cried Peggotty, holding up her hands. "Then there's the sea, and the boats and ships; and the fishermen and the beach; and Am to play with.' She meant her nephew Ham.

David grew quite flushed at the idea, and replied that it would indeed be a treat, but what would his mother say?

"Why then, I'll as good as bet a guinea," said Peggotty, "that she'll let us go. I'll ask her, if you like, as soon as ever she comes home. There, now!"

"But what's she to do while we're away?" asked David. "She can't live by herself."

Peggotty looked quite confused for a moment, and pretended to be looking for another hole in the stocking she was darning.

"I say, Peggotty, she can't live by herself, you know."

"Oh, bless you!" said Peggotty, looking up as if she suddenly remembered. "Don't you know she's going to stay for a fortnight with Mrs Grayper. Mrs Grayper's going to have a lot of company."

Oh! If that was so, David was quite ready to go; and waited in a fever of impatience for his mother's coming home to get leave to carry out this grand idea.

She was not a bit surprised at Peggotty's invitation. Indeed, she seemed to know all about it, and readily entered into the plan.

They were to go in a carrier's cart which left Blunderstone in the morning, after breakfast; for in those days there were no railways at all. And David's box was packed, and Peggotty's box was packed, and when the eventful morning came round, there they were standing at the gate waiting for the carrier's cart; and David's mother was kissing him goodbye, and holding him so close that he felt her heart beat against his. And when the cart arrived, Peggotty and he got in, and as they were moving away his mother ran out of the gate, calling to the carrier to stop that she might kiss her little boy once more.

At last they were off for good, and left her standing in the road; and, looking back, they saw that Mr Murdstone had come up to where she stood, and seemed to be expostulating with her for being so moved; and David, looking round the awning of the cart, wondered what business it was of Mr Murdstone's.

The horse, David thought, was the laziest horse in the world; it shuffled along with its head down; and the carrier held his head down too, like the horse, drooping sleepily forward as he drove, with one of his arms on each of his knees, and whistled a good deal.

Peggotty had a basket of refreshments on her knee, and she and David ate the good things to pass the time away; but the carrier had to call at so many places to deliver his parcels, that David was quite tired, and very glad to see Yarmouth at last.

There were sailors walking about the street, and carts jingling up and down, and there were smells of fish and oakum and tar, and—

"Here's my Am!" screamed Peggotty excitedly, "growed out of knowledge!" as a huge, strong fellow of six feet high, with a boyish face and light, curly hair, stepped out of the door of the public-house where he had been waiting for them.

He caught up David and put him astride his back to carry him home, while he took David's box under his arm. And Peggotty followed with the other box, and they turned down lanes strewn with bits of chips and sand; and went past boat-builders' yards, and ropewalks, and smiths' forges, until they came out upon a flat waste of land across which they could see the sea.

"Yon's our house, Mas'r Davy," said Ham.

"That's not it? That ship-looking thing?" asked David; for he couldn't see any house at all—nothing but a kind of black barge, not far off, high and dry on the ground, with an iron funnel sticking out of it for a chimney, and smoking very cosily.

"That's it, Mas'r Davy," said Ham.

David gasped with pleasure at the romantic idea of living in such a place. There was a delightful door cut in the side, and it was roofed in, and there were little windows in it; but the wonderful charm of it was, that it was a real boat which had no doubt been upon the water hundreds of times, and which had never been intended to be lived in on dry land.

It was beautifully clean inside, and as tidy as possible. There was a table, and a Dutch clock, and on a chest of drawers a tea-tray, which was kept from tumbling down by a Bible, with cups and saucers and a teapot grouped around the book. And there were boxes which served for seats in lieu of chairs, and in the beams of the ceiling were some hooks which David wondered what they were used for.

They were welcomed by a very civil woman in a white apron, and a pretty little girl with a necklace of blue beads on, who wouldn't let David kiss her, but ran away and hid herself.

Then Peggotty opened a little door and showed David his bedroom. It was in the stern of the vessel— the dearest little bedroom ever seen, with a little window where the rudder used to go through; a little looking-glass, just the right height for David, nailed against the wall, and framed with oyster shells; a little bed, which there was just room enough to get into; and a nosegay of seaweed in a blue mug on the table.

They had boiled dabs for dinner, melted butter, and potatoes, with a chop for David; and had just finished when a hairy man with a very good-natured face came in, and was introduced to David as Mr Peggotty, the master of the house, and Peggotty's brother.

"Glad to see you, sir," said Mr Peggotty, "you'll find us rough, sir, but you'll find us ready."

David thanked him, and said he was sure to be happy in such a delightful place.

"How's your Ma, sir?" asked Mr Peggotty. "Did you leave her pretty jolly?"

David said, "Yes," and added that she had sent her compliments to him.

"I'm much obleeged to her, I'm sure," said Mr Peggotty. "Well, sir, if you can make out here for a fortnut long wi' her," nodding at his sister, and Ham, and little Em'ly, we shall be proud of your company"; and Mr Peggotty went out to wash himself with a kettleful of hot water.

After tea the door was shut, and all was made snug, for the nights were cold and misty.

Little Em'ly had overcome her shyness, and sat with David on the lowest locker, which was only large enough for two, and just fitted into the chimney corner. The civil woman with the white apron was knitting on the other side of the fire; and Peggotty with her needlework looked very much at home. Ham was teaching David some tricks with cards, and Mr Peggotty was comfortably smoking his pipe.

"Mr Peggotty," said David by and by.

"sir," said Mr Peggotty.

"Did you give your son the name of Ham, because you lived in a sort of ark?"

"No, sir, I never giv him no name."

"Who gave him that name, then?"

"Why, sir, his father giv it him."

"I thought you were his father," said David.

"My brother Joe was *his* father," said Mr Peggotty.

"Dead, Mr Peggotty?" asked David, after a respectful pause.

"Drowndead," said Mr Peggotty.

David was so surprised, that Mr Peggotty was not Ham's father that he began to wonder next what relation he was to little Em'ly. "Little Em'ly," began David, glancing at her. "She is your daughter, isn't she, Mr Peggotty?"

"No, sir. My brother-in-law, Tom, was *her* father."

"Dead, Mr Peggotty?" asked David after another respectful pause.

"Drowndead," said Mr Peggotty.

"Haven't you any children, Mr Peggotty?"

"No, master. I'm a bacheldore."

"A bachelor!" cried David astonished. "Why, who's that?" pointing to the civil woman with the white apron.

"That's Mrs Gummidge," said Mr Peggotty.

"Gummidge?" began David, when Peggotty—his

own Peggotty—frowned at him to say no more; so David was silent until it was time to go to bed.

And then in the privacy of his own little cabin she told him that Ham and Em'ly were orphans, whom their uncle had adopted when they lost their own parents; and that Mrs Gummidge was the widow of his partner in a boat, who had died very poor, and Mr Peggotty had taken *her* into his house, too, when she was destitute; and that the only thing that ever put Mr Peggotty into a temper was to be reminded of his generosity to her.

David was very much impressed by Mr Peggotty's goodness, and thought about it before he went to sleep.

Peggotty, and Mrs Gummidge, and Little Em'ly went to bed in another little cabin at the opposite end of the boat, and Mr Peggotty and Ham hung up two hammocks for themselves on the hooks that David had seen in the ceiling when he first came in.

He was up early next morning, and out with little Em'ly, picking up stones on the beach.

"You are quite a sailor, I suppose," David said to her. "No," replied Em'ly, shaking her head. "I'm afraid of the sea."

"Afraid!" exclaimed David, looking boldly at the mighty waves. "*I* an't."

"Ah! but it's cruel," said little Em'ly. "I've seen it very cruel to some of our men. I've seen it tear a boat, as big as our house, all to pieces."

"I hope it wasn't the boat that . . ."

"That father was drownded in?" said Em'ly. "No. Not that one. I never see that boat."

"Nor him?" asked David.

Little Em'ly shook her head. "Not to remember," she said.

David told her how he had never seen his father either, and how he and his mother lived by themselves and always meant to do so, for they were very happy. And how his father's grave was in the churchyard near their house, and shaded by a tree.

Em'ly said, that where *her* father's grave was no one knew, except that it was somewhere in the sea.

"Besides," she added, as she looked for shells and pebbles, "your father was a gentleman, and your mother is a lady; and my father was a fisherman and my mother was a fisherman's daughter, and my Uncle Dan is a fisherman too."

"Dan is Mr Peggotty, isn't he?" asked David.

"Uncle Dan—yonder," answered Em'ly, nodding at the boat-house.

"Yes. I mean him. He must be very good," said David, "I should think."

"Good?" said Em'ly. "If I was ever to be a lady, I'd give him a sky-blue coat with diamond buttons, nankeen trousers, a red velvet waistcoat, a cocked hat, a large gold watch, a silver pipe, and a box of money."

They strolled a long way, picking up curious things upon the beach, and went back to breakfast at the boat-house, glowing with health and pleasure.

They became very good friends, and used to walk

about that Yarmouth flat for hours looking for curious things, coming back to the boat-house for meals as hungry as two young thrushes, Mr Peggotty said.

It was a very delightful time.

The only person who didn't make herself so agreeable as she might have done in that romantic little home was Mrs Gummidge.

Mrs Gummidge suffered from low spirits, and alluded to herself as a "lone lorn creetur"; and when her spirits were extra low, hinted oftener than David thought was pleasant, that it would be better for her to go to the workhouse, and die, and be a riddance.

To which Mr Peggotty would answer mildly, "Cheer up, mawther."

"I an't what I could wish myself to be," Mrs Gummidge would say. "I am far from it. I know what I am. My troubles has made me contrairy. I wish I could be hardened to 'em, but I an't. I make the house uncomfortable. I'm a lone lorn creetur, and had much better not make myself contrairy here. If thinks must go contrairy with me, and I must go contrairy myself, let me go contrairy in my parish, Dan'l; I'd better go into the house, and die, and be a riddance."

Then Mrs Gummidge would betake herself to bed, and when David looked at Mr Peggotty, expecting him to be vexed or put out, he would just nod his head with a look of profound sympathy, and whisper, "She 's been thinking of the old 'un."

He meant the late Mr Gummidge. And when he had swung himself into his hammock at night after one of

Mrs Gummidge's contrary fits, David would hear him repeat to himself, "Poor thing! She's been thinking of the old 'un."

Oh! how that fortnight slipped away! When Ham had nothing to do he walked with David and little Em'ly, and showed them the boats and ships, and once or twice he took them for a row. And all too soon the day came at last for going home.

Little Em'ly walked with David to the public-house where the carrier's cart was waiting, and David promised, on the road, to write to her.

They were very sorry to part with each other, for they had become great friends; but they had to say goodbye; and as the carrier's cart started for Blunderstone, David remembered with a thrill of joy that he would see his mother again.

3

Strangers in the Old Home

As they neared the old dear home, and passed familiar places, David grew very much excited, pointing them out to Peggotty, and showing how eager he was to run into his mother's arms.

Peggotty, somehow, did not enter into his transports of joy, and tried to check them quietly, and looked confused and out of sorts.

But Blunderstone Rookery came at last; the carrier pulled up his horse, and David and Peggotty got down.

The door opened, and David, half laughing, half crying, looked up to see his mother; but it was not his mother at the door. It was a strange servant.

"Why, Peggotty!" cried David ruefully, "isn't she come home?"

"Yes, yes, Master Davy," said Peggotty, "she's come home. Wait a bit, Master Davy, and I'll—I'll tell you something."

Peggotty was quite agitated. She took David by the hand, led him into the kitchen, and shut the door.

"Peggotty!" cried he, quite frightened. "What's the matter?"

"Nothing's the matter, bless you, Master Davy dear," answered Peggotty, trying to speak cheerfully.

"Something's the matter, I'm sure. Where's Mamma?"

"Where's Mamma, Master Davy?" repeated Peggotty.

"Yes, why hasn't she come out to the gate, and what have we come in here for? O Peggotty!" He began to tremble.

"Bless the precious boy ! What is it ? Speak, my pet!"

"Not dead, too! Oh, she's not dead, Peggotty?"

Peggotty cried out, "No." And, panting, said that he had given her quite a turn. "You see, dear," she added, when she had become quieter, "I should have told you before now, but I hadn't an opportunity. I ought to have made it, perhaps, but I couldn't azackly bring my mind to it."

"Go on, Peggotty," urged David, more frightened than before.

"Master Davy," said Peggotty, untying her bonnet with a shaking hand, "what do you think? You've got a Pa! A new one!"

"A new one," repeated David.

Peggotty gave a gasp, and putting out her hand, said, "Come and see him."

"I don't want to see him."

"And your Mamma," said Peggotty.

She took him to the best parlour, and left him there. On one side of the fire sat his mother; on the other the gentleman with the black whiskers.

Mrs Copperfield had married Mr Murdstone.

She dropped her work, and rose hurriedly, but timidly, to greet her little boy.

"Now, Clara, my dear," said Mr Murdstone. "Control yourself. Davy boy, how do you do?"

David gave him his hand. After that he went and kissed his mother. She kissed him too, patted him gently on the shoulder, and sat down to her work again, as if she were afraid to show how much she loved her little boy in front of her husband.

David felt quite stunned. He knew that Mr Murdstone was looking at them both, and he turned to the window and looked out there.

As soon as he could creep away, he crept upstairs. Not to the dear old bedroom. He was to have another bedroom now. How altered everything was! It hardly seemed the same old house. He went downstairs, and roamed into the yard; but the empty dog-kennel was filled with a great black dog, that was very angry at the sight of David, and sprang out to get at him.

David ran back to his bedroom, and all the way upstairs he heard the dog barking in the yard. His heart was very heavy; oh! what a homecoming it was!

He sat on the edge of his bed and thought of little Em'ly, and wished they had left him with her, for nobody seemed to want him here. He was very miserable, and at last he rolled himself up in a corner of the counterpane, and cried himself to sleep.

He was awakened at last by a voice saying, "Here

he is," and somebody took the counterpane off his head. Then he saw that his mother and Peggotty had come to look for him.

"Davy," said his mother. "What's the matter?"

David thought it was strange that she should ask him that. He turned over on his face to hide his trembling lips.

"Davy," she said again. "Davy, my child."

But David hid his face in the bedclothes, and pushed her away with his hand.

"Peggotty, this is your doing, you cruel thing," said David's mother, crying out that she had tried to prejudice her boy against her.

"Lord forgive you, Mrs Copperfield," said Peggotty; "and for what you have said this minute, may you never be truly sorry!"

"It's enough to distract me—in my honeymoon, too," said David's mother, "when I might have a little peace of mind and happiness. Davy, you naughty boy! Peggotty!" she cried, turning from one to another in her wilful, girlish way.

Suddenly David felt a touch of a hand that he knew was neither his mother's nor Peggotty's, and he slipped to his feet at the bedside. It was Mr Murdstone's hand, and he kept it on his arm, and said:

"What's this? Clara, my love, have you forgotten? firmness, my dear!"

"I am very sorry, Edward," faltered David's mother. "I meant to be so very good, but I am so uncomfortable."

"Indeed!" said Mr Murdstone. "That's a bad hearing so soon." Then he drew her to him, whispered in her ear, and kissed her, and added, "Go you below, my love; David and I will come down together. My friend," and he turned a darkening face to Peggotty, "do you know your mistress's name?"

"She has been my mistress a long time, sir," said Peggotty, "I ought to know it."

"That's true," he answered. "But as I came upstairs, I heard you address her by a name that is not hers. She has taken mine, you know. Will you remember that?"

Peggotty, with some uneasy glances at David, curtsied herself out of the room, without replying; and when the two were alone, Mr Murdstone sat on a chair and held David standing before him.

"David," he said, "if I have an obstinate horse or dog to deal with, what do you think I do?"

"I don't know."

"I beat him." David gasped. "I make him wince, and smart. What is that upon your face?"

"Dirt," said David; for his childish heart would have burst before he would have confessed that the stains upon his face were tears.

Mr Murdstone smiled. "Wash that face, sir, and come down with me," he said, and pointed to the washstand.

David did so. Then Mr Murdstone walked him down to the parlour, with his hand still on his arm.

"Clara, my dear," he said, "you will not be made uncomfortable any more, I hope. We shall soon improve our youthful humours."

David knew that his mother was sorry to see him look so scared and strange, and when he stole to a chair, he felt her following him with her eyes more sorrowfully still; but she seemed too timid to take him in her arms and kiss him as she would have liked to do.

They dined alone—the three together. Mr Murdstone seemed to be very fond of his pretty young wife, and she of him. David liked him none the better for that. And from their talk he gathered that an elder sister of Mr Murdstone was expected to come and stay with them that evening.

After dinner a coach drove up, and Mr Murdstone went out to receive his sister. Then David's mother caught David in her arms and kissed him tenderly, whispering that he was to love his new father and be obedient to him; and putting her hand behind, held his in hers, and walked out with him like that into the garden.

Miss Murdstone was a gloomy-looking lady; dark, like her brother, whom she greatly resembled in face and voice.

"Is that your boy, sister-in-law?" she asked, when they had brought her into the parlour. "I don't like boys. How d'ye do, boy?"

Miss Murdstone had evidently come for good.

On the very first morning after her arrival she said at breakfast, "Now, Clara, my dear, I am come here, you know, to relieve you of all the trouble I can. You're much too pretty and thoughtless to have any duties imposed upon you that can be undertaken by me. If you'll be so good as to give me your keys, my dear, I'll attend to all this sort of thing in future."

So the keys were handed over to Miss Murdstone, and she went about turning out the storeroom and all the cupboards, arranging everything according to *her* liking; and kept her brother's wife in the background quite.

David's mother didn't like it very much, and tried to protest; and at last she burst out one day, "It's very hard that in my own house—"

"*My* own house?" repeated Mr Murdstone, "Clara!"

"Our own house, I mean," she faltered, evidently frightened. "It's very hard that in *your* own house, Edward, I may not have a word to say about domestic matters. I am sure I managed very well before we were married."

"Edward," said Miss Murdstone, "let there be an end of this. I go tomorrow."

At that Mr Murdstone was very angry, and David's mother cried, and in the end she begged Miss Murdstone's pardon, and humbly asked her to keep the keys, and kissed her, and tried to make friends.

David was so sorry for his mother that he cried himself to sleep. And after that the poor little wife left the management of her whole house in Miss Murdstone's hands, and never protested again.

David used to wonder, as they walked home from

church—Mr and Miss Murdstone in front, with the little wife between them, and David himself lagging behind—if the neighbours ever called to mind, as he did often, how he and his mother used to walk home hand-in-hand so loving and happy together. All gone was that happy time!

He used to notice the neighbours whispering sometimes, and looking from her to him. And when he looked at her he thought that her step was not so light as it used to be, and that her once girlish face had a worried, saddened look.

He learned his lessons with his mother as he used to do, but as Mr and Miss Murdstone were generally in the room their presence made him nervous, and the geography or spelling that he had taken such pains to learn would all fly out of his head, and he would stumble and make mistakes.

He used to think, at those times, that if his mother had dared she would have shown him the book; indeed, sometimes she would try to give him the cue by mouthing the words at him.

"Clara!" The exclamation would break from Mr Murdstone; and David's mother would start, and colour, and try to smile.

Then Mr Murdstone would take the book from her, and throw it at David, or box his ears with it, or turn him out by the shoulders.

This kind of treatment made David sullen, and dull, and dogged; especially as the Murdstones kept him away from his mother when they could. He had one comfort, however, which the Murdstones knew nothing about—a pleasure, too, which they could not rob him of.

It was this. In a little room upstairs, adjoining his, to which he could go when he liked, he found a collection of books that his dead father had owned. Oh! those blessed books ! Whenever he was in trouble he stole up and read these books—such books!— *Roderick Random, Peregrine Pickle, Humphry Clinker, Robinson Crusoe, The Arabian Nights*, and a host of others that he got to know by heart. And in his childish way he would imagine himself Roderick Random, or play at Robinson Crusoe, and get a great deal of comfort thereby.

One morning when he went into the parlour with his books, he found his mother looking very anxious, while Mr Murdstone was switching a cane in the air, and David heard him say, "I've often been flogged myself."

Of course that made David more nervous and more stupid than ever, and he began to make many mistakes in his lessons. Lesson after lesson was put aside for him to learn over again, until his mother burst out crying.

"Clara!" said Miss Murdstone in a warning voice.

"I am not quite well, I think," faltered the mother.

"David," said Mr Murdstone, taking up the cane, "you and I will go upstairs, boy."

The mother stretched out her arms and ran after them to the door; but Miss Murdstone stopped her, and David saw her put her fingers into her ears, and heard her sob.

Mr Murdstone took David upstairs, and when they reached his room, he caught David's head under his arm.

"Mr Murdstone! sir!" cried David. "Don't! Pray don't beat me! I have tried to learn, sir, but I can't learn while you and Miss Murdstone are by. I can't indeed."

"Can't you, indeed, David?" he said. "We'll try that."

Then the cane went up and cut down heavily, and in the same instant David caught Mr Murdstone's hand between his teeth, and bit it through.

He beat him then as if he would have beaten him to death. David screamed, and he heard the others running upstairs. He heard his mother crying out—and Peggotty.

Then Mr Murdstone left him alone and locked the door, and David fell down sobbing, and sore, and raging upon the floor.

After a while his passion began to cool, and he began to think he had been very wicked to have bitten Mr Murdstone's hand. He sat listening; but could not hear a sound. Then he crawled up from the floor, and looked at his face in the glass, so swollen, and red, and blotched; and he was so sore and stiff from the beating that to move was real pain; but he crawled up to the window and laid his head upon the sill, and looked out listlessly, and cried and dozed in turns.

The room was getting dark when the key of the door was turned, and Miss Murdstone stalked in with some bread, and meat, and milk. She did not say a word, only looked at him very coldly; then she went out again and locked the door.

He sat there till it grew quite dark, wondering whether anyone else would come; and then he undressed and crept to bed. He began to be afraid, as he lay there, at what he had done, and wondered what they were going to do to him.

Was it a crime that he had committed? And would a policeman come for him to take him away to prison? He could not tell.

Miss Murdstone appeared again next morning before he was out of bed, and told him coldly that he was at liberty to walk for half an hour in the garden. After that he had to go back to his room again; and in the evening she came and escorted him down to the parlour for family prayers, where he had to kneel down far away from the others, near the door. His mother was not allowed to speak to him; and Mr Murdstone's hand was bound up in a large linen wrapper.

If he could have seen his mother alone he would have gone on his knees to beg her forgiveness; but he never saw her alone. For five days he was kept a prisoner in his room, and on the fifth night, after he had gone to bed, he was awakened by hearing his name spoken in a whisper. He started up, and groping his way to the door he put his mouth to the keyhole, whispering, "Is that you, Peggotty, dear?"

"Yes, my own precious Davy," she replied. "Be as soft as a mouse, or the Cat will hear us."

David knew that she meant Miss Murdstone. "How's Mamma, dear Peggotty? Is she very angry with me?"

Peggotty was crying softly on the other side of the keyhole. "No. Not very," she said.

"What is going to be done with me, Peggotty, do you know?"

"School. Near London," came Peggotty's whisper through the keyhole.

"When, Peggotty?"

"Tomorrow."

"Shan't I see Mamma?"

"Yes," whispered Peggotty. "Morning." Then she put her mouth close to the keyhole, saying in disjointed sentences. "Davy, dear. If I an't ben exactly as intimate with you. Lately as I used to be. It ain't because I don't love you. Just as much and more, my pretty poppet. It's because I thought it better for you. And for someone else besides. Davy, my darling, are you listening? Can you hear?"

"Ye—ye—yes, Peggotty," he sobbed.

"My own," said Peggotty with infinite compassion. "What I want to say is. That you must never forget me. For I'll never forget you. And I'll take as much care of your Mamma, Davy. As I ever took of you. And I won't ever leave her. And I'll write to you, my dear. And I'll—I'll" Peggotty fell to kissing the keyhole, as she could not kiss David himself.

"Thank you, dear Peggotty. Oh, thank you! Thank you. Will you promise me one thing, Peggotty? Will you write and tell Mr Peggotty and little Em'ly, and Mrs Gummidge and Ham, that I'm not so bad as they might suppose, and that I sent them all my love—especially to little Em'ly? Will you, if you please, Peggotty?"

Good, kind Peggotty promised, and they both kissed the keyhole with the greatest affection.

In the morning Miss Murdstone appeared as usual, and told David he was going to school. David did not tell her it was stale news.

He went down with her to the parlour where he was to have his breakfast; and there he found his mother very pale, and with red eyes. David ran into her arms, and begged her to forgive him.

"O Davy!" she said, "that you could hurt anyone that I love! Try to be better. I forgive you; but I am so grieved, Davy, that you should have such bad passions in your heart."

For the Murdstones had made out to her that David was a wicked fellow, not worthy of her pity and love. He tried to eat his breakfast, but the tears dropped upon his bread-and-butter, and trickled into his tea. He saw his mother looking at him yearningly, but Miss Murdstone looked at her, and then she looked away.

Presently wheels were heard at the gate. He heard Miss Murdstone say, "Master Copperfield's box there!" and Barkis, the carrier, came and lifted it up and put it into his cart.

"Goodbye, Davy. You are going for your own good," said his mother, holding him. "Goodbye, my child. I forgive you, my dear boy. God bless you."

"Clara!" interrupted Miss Murdstone. His mother let him go, and Miss Murdstone conducted him to the cart and said that she hoped that he would repent, before he came to a bad end. David couldn't see Peggotty anywhere, and Mr Murdstone did not appear.

He got into the cart, and the lazy horse that had taken him that happy day to Yarmouth, walked off in his shuffling way.

4

Travelling by Coach

They might have gone about half a mile when the carrier suddenly stopped short. And David, looking out to see why he didn't go on, saw Peggotty run down from behind a hedge, and climb up into the cart.

She took him in her arms and kissed and hugged him; but was panting too much to say a single word. Then releasing one of her arms, she put it down into her pocket to the elbow, and brought out some paper bags of cakes, which she crammed into David's pockets, and a purse which she put into his hand. Then she gave him another squeeze and got down from the cart and ran away.

"Come up," said the carrier to the lazy horse, and the horse shuffled on again.

David cried until he could cry no more, and Barkis, looking at him, suggested that his wet handkerchief should be spread upon the horse's back to dry. David gave it to him, and the carrier spread it there; and David, looking into the purse that Peggotty had given him, found three bright shillings in it. And in another compartment he found two half-crowns wrapped up in a piece of paper on which was written in his mother's hand, "For Davy, with my love."

David was so overcome that he began to cry again, and asked the carrier to reach him his handkerchief from the horse's back. But Barkis said he thought he was better without, so David wiped his eyes on his sleeves instead, and stopped crying.

Then they had a little talk, and Barkis said he was only going as far as Yarmouth. "And there," he said, "I shall take you to the stage-cutch, and the stage-cutch that'll take you to—wherever it is."

David then offered Barkis one of his cakes, which he ate at one gulp, just like an elephant. "Did *she* make 'em, now?" asked the carrier, leaning forward in his slouching way.

"Peggotty, do you mean?"

"Ah!" said Barkis. "Her."

"Yes. She makes all our pastry and does all the cooking."

"Do she though," said Barkis. He made up his mouth to whistle, but he didn't whistle, and looked at the horse's ears.

"No sweethearts, I believe?" he asked after a considerable time.

"Sweatmeats, did you say, Mr Barkis?" said David, thinking he wanted something more to eat.

"Hearts," said Barkis, "sweethearts; no person walks with her!"

"With Peggotty?"

"Ah! Her."

"Oh, no. She never had a sweetheart."

"Didn't she though," said Barkis. Again he made up his mouth to whistle, and again he didn't whistle, but sat looking at the horse's ears.

"So she makes all the apple parsties, and does all the cooking, do she?"

David said yes.

"Well, I'll tell you what," said Barkis. "P'raps you might be writing to her?"

David nodded.

"Ah!" he said slowly, turning his eyes on him. "Well! If you was writin' to her, p'raps you'd recollect to say that Barkis is willin'; would you?"

"That Barkis is willing. Is that all the message?"

"Ye—es," he said, considering. "Ye—es. Barkis is willin'."

"'But you'll be at Blunderstone again tomorrow, Mr Barkis, and could give your own message so much better."

But Barkis only shook his head and repeated, "'Barkis is willin'.' That's the message."

So while they were waiting in the hotel at Yarmouth for the coach, David got a sheet of paper and an ink-stand, and wrote this letter to Peggotty:

"My dear Peggotty. I have come here safe. Barkis is willing. My love to Mamma. Yours affectionately. P. S. He says he particularly wants you to know— *Barkis is willing*."

By and by the mistress of the hotel asked if that was the little gentleman from Blunderstone, and having discovered it was so, she rang a bell and called to a waiter to take David to the coffee-room.

The waiter took him into a large, long room and laid a cloth, and brought in some chops and vegetables, put a chair for David at the table, and said affably, "Now, six foot! Come on!"

David took his seat, but was so abashed at the waiter standing opposite and staring at him that he splashed himself with the gravy, and blushed very much.

"There's half a pint of ale for you," said the waiter. "Will you have it now?"

David thanked him, and said, "Yes." Upon which he poured it out of a jug into a large tumbler, and held it up against the light.

"My eye!" he said, "it seems a good deal, don't it?"

David agreed, and felt quite pleased to find him such a pleasant man.

"There was a gentleman here yesterday," he said, "a stout gentleman, by the name of Topsawyer; perhaps you know him?"

"No," said David.

"In breeches and gaiters, broad-brimmed hat, speckled choker," said the waiter.

"No," repeated David bashfully.

"He come in here," said the waiter, "ordered a glass of this ale—*would* order it—I told him not—drank it, and fell dead."

David was much startled, and said he thought he had better have some water.

"Why, you see," said the waiter, looking at the tum-

bler with one of his eyes shut up, "our people don't
like things being ordered and then left. It offends 'em.
But I'll drink it, if you like. I'm used to it, and use is
everything. I don't think it'll hurt me, if I throw my
head back, and take it off quick. Shall I?"

David said if he was sure it wouldn't hurt him, he
would be very much obliged to him. And when the
waiter did throw his head back, and take it off quick,
David watched him in some alarm lest he, too, should
fall down dead. But it didn't hurt him.

Indeed, on the contrary, the waiter seemed the
fresher for it.

"What have we got here?" said he, putting a fork
into the dish. "Not chops?"

"Chops," said David.

"Lord bless my soul!" he exclaimed. "I didn't know
they were chops. Why, a chop's the very thing to take
off the bad effects of that beer! Ain't it lucky?"

So he took a chop by the bone in one hand, and a
potato in the other, and ate away with a very good appetite.

After the chops were finished, he brought a pudding, and putting it before David, he appeared to become absent in his mind for some moments.

"How's the pie?" he said suddenly.

"It's a pudding," said David.

"Pudding!" he exclaimed. "Why, bless me, so it is.
What!" looking at it nearer, "you don't mean to say
it's a batter pudding!"

"Yes, it is, indeed."

"Why, a batter pudding," he said, taking up a table-spoon, "is my favourite pudding! Ain't that lucky! Come on, little 'un, and let's see who'll get most."

The waiter certainly got most. He entreated David more than once to come in and win, but what with his tablespoon to David's teaspoon, and his appetite to David's appetite, the small boy was left far behind.

By and by the blowing of the coach horn sounded in the yard; and when David was being helped up behind the coach, he heard the mistress of the hotel say to the guard, "Take care of that child, George, or he'll burst!" And then some of the women servants of the hotel came out to look at him, and giggled.

They thought he had eaten all the chops and all the potatoes in the dish, and the whole of the batter pudding himself.

And when the coachman had cracked his whip and they were well on their way, he and the guard had some jokes about the coach drawing heavy behind, on account of David's sitting there, and suggested that he ought to have travelled by wagon.

Then the outside passengers got hold of the story of his supposed large appetite, and asked David whether he was going to be paid for at school as two brothers or three and were very merry over it indeed.

Poor David was so ashamed, that when the coach stopped for the passengers to have supper at another hotel, he pretended he was not hungry at all, and did not take any supper, though he would have liked some very much. This did not save him from more jokes, however, for an old gentleman said he was like a boa constrictor, that took enough at one meal to last him for a long time.

In those days, as I explained before, there were no railways at all, and people journeying from one place to another always travelled by coach.

They had left Yarmouth at three o'clock in the afternoon, and would not reach London till eight the next morning. It was fine summer weather though, and the evening was very pleasant. David liked driving through the villages one after another, and tried to picture to himself what the insides of the houses were like. Sometimes boys came running after them and swung on to the coach for a little while, and David wondered whether their fathers were alive, and whether they were happy at home. He thought a good deal, too, of his mother and Peggotty, but it seemed ages since he had left Blunderstone.

Morning came at last, and by and by great, busy, bustling London came in sight, and in due time the coach reached its destination at an inn, somewhere in the Whitechapel district.

"Is there anybody here for a youngster booked in the name of Murdstone, from Bloonderstone, Soof-folk, to be left till called for?" asked the guard at the booking Office.

Nobody answered.

"Try Copperfield, if you please, sir, said David.

The guard repeated his question, adding, "But owning to the name of Copperfield."

No, there was nobody.

And a facetious man in gaiters suggested that they should put a brass collar round David's neck, and tie him up in the stable.

Then a ladder was brought, and all the passengers got down, and the luggage was cleared away, and the horses were taken out of the coach. Still nobody appeared to claim the dusty youngster from Blunderstone, Suffolk.

David went into the booking-office, and the clerk let him sit on the scale where all the luggage was weighed; and the little fellow sat looking at the parcels, and wondering what would happen to him suppose nobody were to come for him.

5

First Weeks at Salem House

At last a gaunt, sallow young man, with hollow
cheeks, dressed in a suit of rusty black, rather short in
the sleeves and legs, came into the office and whispered to the clerk, who slanted David off the scale
and pushed him over to the newcomer. He took hold
of David's hand, and the two went out together.

"You're the new boy," he said. "I'm one of the masters at Salem House."

David made him a bow and felt very much over-
awed; and was so ashamed to mention such a com-
monplace thing as his box, to a scholar and a master
at Salem House, that they had gone some distance before he had the courage to allude to it. So they went
back to the office, and the master told the clerk that
the carrier would call for it at noon.

"If you please, sir," asked David, when they were
on their way again, "is it far?"

"It's down by Blackheath," he said.

"Is that far, sir?" asked David.

"It's a good step," he said. "We shall go by the
stagecoach. It's about six miles."

David felt so tired and faint, for he had eaten nothing since the waiter had helped him with his chops

and batter pudding yesterday, that he took heart to tell the master so.

The Master then said that he wanted to call on an old person not far off, and that if David bought something on the way he could eat it at her house.

So they bought a nice little loaf of brown bread at a baker's shop; and then got an egg and a slice of streaky bacon at a grocer's, and David carried them until they came to the poor person's house, which, David saw at once, was a part of some almshouses.

The Master lifted the latch of one of a number of little black doors that were all alike, and they went into the little house of a poor old woman who was blowing a fire to make a little saucepan boil.

As soon as she saw the Master she cried out something like "My Charley!" but on seeing David come in too, she got up and made a confused sort of curtsy.

"Can you cook this young gentleman's breakfast for him, if you please?" said the Master at Salem House.

"Can I?" said the old woman. "Yes, can I, sure." And she cooked it very nicely indeed.

While David was enjoying his meal, the old woman said, "Have you got your flute with you?"

"Yes," answered the Master.

"Have a blow at it," said the old woman, coaxingly. "Do."

So the Master pulled out his flute in three pieces, which he screwed together, and immediately began to play.

David thought that the tune he played was a very

dismal one and most melancholy, so melancholy, indeed, that it first brought tears into his eyes, and then made him go to sleep. And while he was dozing he had a fancy that the old woman crept nearer the Master until she was close enough to give him an affectionate squeeze round the neck.

But he woke up by and by, and the Master unscrewed his flute and put the pieces away; and told David it was time to go for the coach.

It was not far off, and they got upon the roof; but David was so sleepy that when they stopped on the road to take up somebody else, they put him inside the coach where there were no passengers, and he slept sound.

The coach stopped by and by, and the Master fetched him out, and a short walk brought them to a dull-looking place with a high brick wall all round, and over a door in the wall was a board with SALEM HOUSE upon it; and through a grating in the door a surly face peered at them when they rang the bell, and a short man with a bull-neck, a wooden leg, and his hair cut close all round his head, opened the door.

"The new boy," said the Master.

The man with the wooden leg eyed David over, and locked the gate behind them, and shouted, "Hallo!" when they had gone towards the house.

They looked back, and the man, who was standing at the door of a little lodge with a pair of boots in his hand, said, "Here! The cobbler's been, since you've been out, Mr Mell, and he says he can't mend 'em any more. He says there ain't a bit of the original boot left, and he wonders you expect it." Then he threw the boots towards Mr Mell, who picked them up, and looked at them very disconsolately. And David then noticed for the first time that the boots he had on were very much the worse for wear.

There was not a sound about the place. It was so quiet that David asked if the boys were all out.

Then Mr Mell explained to him that it was holiday time, and that the boys were all at their homes, and that Mr Creakle, the proprietor, was at the seaside with Mrs and Miss Creakle; and that David was sent there in holiday time as a punishment for having bitten Mr Murdstone.

The schoolroom was the most desolate place David had ever seen—a long room with three long rows of desks, and six forms splashed all over with ink.

Mr Mell left him there while he carried his boots upstairs, and David, looking round the room, suddenly espied a pasteboard placard, beautifully written, which was lying on the desk, and bore these words: *"Take care of him. He bites."*

At that he got upon the desk immediately and looked round with anxious eyes for the dog, but couldn't see him; and then Mr Mell came in, and asked what he was doing up there.

"I beg your pardon, sir," said David. "If you please, I'm looking for the dog."

"Dog?" said Mr Mell. "What dog?"

"Isn't it a dog, sir?"

"Isn't what a dog?"

"That's to be taken care of, sir; that bites."

"No, Copperfield," said Mr Mell gravely, "that's not a dog. That's a boy. My instructions are, Copperfield, to put this placard on your back. I am sorry to make such a beginning with you, but I must do it."

With that he took David down, and tied the placard like a knapsack on his shoulders.

Poor David! What he suffered from that placard nobody can imagine. He knew that the servants read it, and the butcher read it; that everybody that came to the house of a morning when he was ordered to walk in the playground, which was a bare gravelled yard at the back of the house, read that he was to be taken care of, as he bit. And whenever the man with the wooden leg saw him lean against the wall to hide it, he would roar out in a cruel voice:

"Hallo, you sir! You Copperfield! Show that badge conspicuous, or I'll report you!"

David had long tasks to do with Mr Mell every day; but, as neither Mr nor Miss Murdstone was there to make him nervous, he did them without disgrace.

He and Mr Mell dined at one, at the end of a long, bare dining-room. Then he had more tasks till tea, and walked afterwards in the playground, overlooked by the man with the wooden leg.

Mr Mell never said much to him, but he was never harsh to David. And when he went to bed among the unused rooms full of empty beds, he couldn't help crying sometimes for a comfortable word from Peggotty.

There was an old door in the playground, on which the boys had a custom of carving their names. It was completely covered with them. And as David read the names he couldn't help wondering how each boy would read the placard on his back, *"Take care of him He bites."*

There was one boy—a certain J. Steerforth—who cut his name very deep, who, David imagined, would read it in rather a strong voice, and afterwards pull his hair. And there was another, Tommy Traddles, who, he dreaded, would make game of it, and pretend to be dreadfully frightened of him.

There were forty-five boys in all, Mr Mell told him, and though he longed often for their companionship he dreaded their coming to read, *"Take care of him. He bites."*

6

J. Steerforth and Traddles

David had lead this life for about a month, when the man with the wooden leg began to stump about with a mop and a bucket of water, and David was always in the way of two or three women brushing and dusting about. Then one day Mr Mell told him that Mr Creakle would be home in the evening; and that night before his bedtime the man with the wooden leg came and fetched him to appear before Mr Creakle.

David was taken into the parlour, but he was trembling so much that he hardly saw Mrs and Miss Creakle, who were sitting there, or anything but Mr Creakle—a stout gentleman with a bunch of watch chain and seals, in an armchair, with a tumbler and bottle beside him.

"So!" said Mr Creakle. "This is the young gentleman whose teeth are to be filed! Turn him round!"

The wooden-legged man turned him round so as to show the placard, then turned him about again with his face to Mr Creakle, and posted himself at Mr Creakle's side.

Mr Creakle's face was fiery, and his eyes were small and deep in his head; he had a little nose, and a large chin; but what impressed David most was the fact that he had no voice, for he spoke in a whisper.

"Now," said Mr Creakle, "what's the report of this boy?"

"There's nothing against him yet," said the man with the wooden leg.

Mr Creakle looked disappointed. Mrs and Miss Creakle, who were both thin and quiet, looked pleased.

"Come here, sir," said Mr Creakle, beckoning to David.

"I have the happiness of knowing your stepfather," said Mr Creakle in his whisper, taking him by the ear; "and a very worthy man he is, and a man of strong character. He knows me, and I know him. Do you know me? Hey?" said Mr Creakle, pinching his ear.

"Not yet, sir," said David, flinching with the pain.

"Not yet? Hey? But you will soon, hey?"

"You will soon, hey?" repeated the man with the wooden leg. And David afterwards found that he generally acted, with his strong voice, as Mr Creakle's interpreter to the boys.

David was very much frightened, and said, he hoped so, if he pleased.

"I'll tell you what I am," whispered Mr Creakle, letting his ear go at last, with a parting pinch that brought the tears into his eyes, "I'm a Tartar."

"A Tartar," repeated the man with the wooden leg.

"When I say I'll do a thing, I do it," said Mr Creakle, "and when I say I will have a thing done, I will have it done."

"—Will have a thing done, I will have it done," repeated the man with the wooden leg, like an echo.

After that Mr Creakle ordered him away, and David, wondering at his own courage, blurted out, "If you please, sir—"

"Hah?" whispered Mr Creakle, "what's this?"

"If you please, sir, if I might be allowed (I am very sorry indeed, sir, for what I did) to take this writing off, before the boys come back—"

Mr Creakle made a burst out of his chair, and David without waiting for the man with the wooden leg, fled out of the room, and never stopped till he reached his own bedroom; and getting into bed he lay quaking there for a couple of hours.

Next morning Mr Sharp came back. Mr Sharp was the first master, and superior to Mr Mell. Mr Mell took his meals with the boys, but Mr Sharp dined and supped at Mr Creakle's table. He was a limp, delicate-looking man, with a good deal of nose, and a lot of smooth, wavy hair.

The first boy that returned was Tommy Traddles. He introduced himself to David by saying that he would find his name on the right-hand corner of the gate, over the top bolt.

"Traddles?" said David.

"The same," said Traddles. And then he asked for a full account of David and his family; and informed him that Mr Sharp's hair was not his own, but that he wore a wig (a second-hand one), and that Mr Sharp went out every Saturday afternoon to get it curled.

It was a happy thing for David that Traddles arrived first. He enjoyed the placard very much, and saved David from embarrassment by presenting him to every other boy that came back, in this form of introduction.

"Look here! Here's a game."

Some of the boys danced around him like wild Indians, and some called him "Towser," and others patted him, and said, "Lie down, sir," but the greater part of the boys were so low-spirited at having to return, that they were not as merry at David's expense as they might otherwise have been.

J. Steerforth hadn't come yet. The boys spoke of him as a clever fellow and very handsome, and David was not considered as being formally received into the school till J. Steerforth arrived.

He turned up at last; he was about six years older than David, and the new boy was taken to him as before a magistrate.

Under a shed in the playground Steerforth examined the placard, and inquired into the particulars of David's punishment.

David told him all about Mr Murdstone and how he had bitten his hand.

Whereupon J. Steerforth said that the placard was "A jolly shame," which bound David to him ever after.

"What money have you got, Copperfield?" asked Steerforth, taking him aside.

David told him seven shillings.

"You had better give it to me to take care of," he

said; "at least you can if you like. You needn't if you don't like."

David immediately opened Peggotty's purse, and turned it upside down into his hand.

"Do you want to spend anything now?" he asked.

"No, thank you," said David.

"You can if you like, you know," said Steerforth. "Say the word."

"No, thank you," repeated David.

"Perhaps you'd like to spend a couple of shillings or so in a bottle of currant wine by and by, up in the bedroom. You belong to my bedroom, I find."

Davie said he would like that.

"Very good," said Steerforth. "You'll be glad to spend another shilling or so in almond cakes, I dare say?"

David thought he would like that too.

"And another shilling in biscuits, and another in fruit, eh?" said Steerforth. I say, young Copperfield, you're going it!"

He smiled, and David couldn't help smiling too.

"Well," said Steerforth, "we must make it stretch as far as we can; that's all. I'll do the best in my power for you. I can go out when I like, and I'll smuggle the prog in." Then he put the money into his pocket and kindly told David that he'd take care it should be all right.

He was as good as his word: for when they went upstairs to bed he produced the whole seven shillings worth, and laid it out on David's bed in the moonlight, saying:

"There you are, young Copperfield, and a royal spread you've got!"

David couldn't dream of doing the honours of the feast while this clever, handsome fellow was by, so he begged Steerforth to preside. The other boys in the bedroom seconded David's wish, and Steerforth gracefully acceded to it, and sat upon the pillow, handing round the cakes and fruits with perfect fairness, indeed, and dispensing the currant wine in a little glass without a foot, which was his own property; while David sat on his left hand, with the others grouped around them.

They all spoke in whispers; and when Steerforth wanted to look for anything, he dipped a match into a phosphorus-box and shed a blue glare that was gone in a second.

They told the new boy in whispers all about the school; that Mr Creakle was the sternest and most severe of masters; and that he laid about him, right and left, every day of his life. That he had taken to the schooling business after being bankrupt in hops, and that he had made away with Mrs Creakle's money. That the man with the wooden leg, whose name was Tungay, had been in the hop business too, and had broken his leg in Mr Creakle's service. That Mr Creakle had a son, who had not been Tungay's friend, and who, for interfering with his father's harsh treatment in the school, had been turned out of doors: and that Mrs and Miss Creakle had been sad ever since.

He heard also that Mr Sharp and Mr Mell were both

supposed to be wretchedly paid; that Mr Mell was not a bad sort of fellow, but hadn't a sixpence to bless himself with; and that old Mrs Mell, his mother, was as poor as Job. David suddenly remembered the old woman who had cried, "My Charley!" when he went to have his breakfast cooked, but he didn't tell that to the others.

And he heard, too, that Miss Creakle was supposed by all the boys to be in love with Steerforth, which he didn't wonder at at all; and that Steerforth was a parlour boarder, the son of a very rich lady, and the only boy in the school on whom Mr Creakle never ventured to lay a hand. After that the boys dispersed and betook themselves to bed.

David thought a great deal of Steerforth after he went to bed, and raised himself on his elbow to look at him lying in the moonlight with his handsome face turned up, and his head reclining on his arm.

"Goodnight, young Copperfield," he had said before he went to sleep. "I'll take care of you."

And David in his gratitude and admiration looked up to him as a hero and a king.

7

School Life

School began in earnest next day.

The roar of voices in the schoolroom suddenly became as hushed as death when Mr Creakle came in, and stood in the doorway looking round upon the boys, and crying in a ferocious whisper, "Silence!"

Tungay stood at his elbow, repeating in his strong voice what Mr Creakle said in a whisper.

"Now, boys, this is a new half. Take care what you're about in this new half. Come fresh up to the lessons, I advise you, for I come fresh up to the punishment. I won't flinch. It will be no use your rubbing yourselves; you won't rub the marks out of that which I shall give you. Now get to work, every boy!"

Then Tungay stumped out, and Mr Creakle came to where David sat, and told him that if he were famous for biting, Mr Creakle was famous for biting too. He then showed David the cane, and asked him what he thought of that for a tooth? Was it a sharp tooth, hey? Was it a double tooth, hey? Did it bite, hey? And at every question, he gave David a cut with it that made him writhe.

But he was not the only boy that was caned that day; half the school was writhing and crying before the day's work was done, and Mr Creakle seemed to enjoy his share of it very much.

He was an ignorant and cruel man, whose sole duty and pleasure consisted in punishing the boys. The teaching was left to Mr Sharp and Mr Mell.

Poor Traddles was a most unfortunate boy, and got caned every day that half-year; but he was the merriest if he was the most miserable of the boys, and after laying his head on the desk for a little while he would cheer up somehow, begin to laugh again, and draw skeletons all over his slate, before his eyes were dry.

He was very honourable, Traddles was; and held it a solemn duty in the boys to stand by one another. Once Steerforth laughed in church, and the beadle thought it was Traddles, and took him out. He never said who was the real offender, though he smarted for it the next day. But he had his reward. Steerforth said there was nothing of the sneak in Traddles, and the boys all felt that to be the highest praise.

Steerforth continued his protection of David, and proved a very useful friend; because nobody dared to annoy one whom he honoured with his friendship. Once, when they were talking in the playground, David happened to say something about one of his beloved books, *Peregrine Pickle;* and that night when they were going to bed Steerforth asked him if he had that book with him.

David said no, and explained how he had come to read it, and all those other dear books which he had found in that little upstairs room next his.

"And do you recollect them?" Steerforth asked.

David thought he did.

"Then I'll tell you what, young Copperfield, you shall tell 'em to me. I can't get to sleep very early at night, and I generally wake rather early in the morning. We'll go over 'em one after another. We'll make some regular Arabian Nights of it.

David felt very much flattered, and began on Peregrine Pickle that very evening, after they were in bed. He didn't like being roused out of sleep in the mornings to go on with the story, but Steerforth kept him at it with the greatest zest; and David admired him so much that he would not have disappointed him for the world.

And one day Peggotty's promised letter came at last —such a comfortable letter, just like Peggotty! And with it a cake, a lot of oranges, and two bottles of cowslip wine.

These treasures David, as in duty bound, laid at Steerforth's feet, and begged him to send them round.

"Now I'll tell you what, young Copperfield,' said he, "the wine shall be kept to wet your whistle when you're storytelling."

David tried to object; but Steerforth was firm. He had observed, he said that David was "a little roopy," and declared that every drop of the wine should be kept for him.

So Steerforth locked the bottles up in his own box, and used to draw a little in a phial whenever David became "roopy." Sometimes he squeezed orange juice into it for a change, or stirred it up with ginger, or dissolved a peppermint drop in it; and David drank it very gratefully, and was very sensible of his attention.

David told the stories very well, because he believed in them so earnestly himself. He was the youngest boy in that bedroom too, and for that very reason, perhaps, the boys thought more of this accomplishment of his. The whole school gradually got to know of it, and David was a good deal noticed in consequence.

The old placard had been taken off his back by this—not from any consideration of David's feelings; Mr Creakle found it in his way when he came suddenly behind the form where David sat, and wanted to make a cut at him when passing; for this reason it was taken off one day, and never put on again.

Mr Mell, too, got a liking for him, and did his best to teach him very carefully. Unfortunately, David, who could not have kept a secret from Steerforth for the world, told his hero once about the old woman whom Mr Mell had taken him to see at the almshouse that first morning. He little guessed what the consequence would be.

Mr Creakle was ill one day, and couldn't come to the schoolroom. The boys became so lively at the news, that it was very hard to keep them in order that morning. Tungay stumped in with his wooden leg, and took down the names of the principal offenders; but they were so sure of getting punished tomorrow that they thought they would enjoy themselves today.

They became worse in the afternoon—it happened to be Saturday afternoon, which was generally a half holiday; but as Mr Creakle could not bear the noise of the boys rushing about the playground, and the day being too wet for walking out, they were ordered into the schoolroom to do a few light tasks, under the care of Mr Mell. Mr Sharp had gone out to get his wig curled.

The boys were so rowdy that poor Mr Mell, who was a quiet, mild man, had the utmost difficulty in keeping order. The noise was fearful.

He leaned his aching head on his hand and tried to get on with his tiresome work as well as he could.

Boys started in and out of their places, playing at puss-in-the-corner with the other boys; there were laughing boys, singing boys, talking boys, howling boys; boys shuffled with their feet, boys whirled about him, grinning, making faces, mimicking him behind his back and before his eyes; mimicking his poverty, his boots, his coat, his mother; everything belonging to him that they should have had consideration for.

"Silence!" cried Mr Mell, suddenly rising up, and striking the desk with his book. "What does this mean? It is impossible to bear it. It's maddening. How can you do it to me, boys?"

It was David's book that he struck the desk with; and David was standing by his side.

All the boys stopped, some suddenly surprised, some half afraid, some sorry, perhaps.

Steerforth's place was at the bottom of the school, at the opposite side of the long room. He was lounging with his back against the wall, and his hands in his pockets, and looked at Mr Mell with his mouth shut up as if he were whistling, when Mr Mell looked at him.

"Silence, Steerforth!" said Mr Mell.

"Silence yourself," said Steerforth, very red. "Whom are you talking to?"

"Sit down," said Mr Mell.

"Sit down yourself," said Steerforth, "and mind your own business."

Some of the boys tittered; some applauded; but Mr Mell grew so white that silence immediately succeeded.

"If you think, Steerforth," said Mr Mell, "that I am not acquainted with the power you can stretch over any mind here; or that I have not observed you, within a few minutes, urging your juniors on to every sort of outrage against me; you are mistaken."

"I don't give myself the trouble of thinking at all about you," said Steerforth, who was proud of his own position, and looked down on Mr Mell: "so I am not mistaken, as it happens."

"And when you make use of your position of favouritism here, sir," went on Mr Mell, with his lip trembling very much, "to insult a gentleman——"

"A what? Where is he?" cried Steerforth.

Here somebody cried out, "Shame, J. Steerforth Too bad!" It was Traddles.

"—To insult one who is not fortunate in life, sir, and who never gave you the least offence," said Mr Mell, with his lips trembling more and more, "you commit a mean and base action. You can sit down or stand up as you please, sir. Copperfield, go on."

"Young Copperfield," said Steerforth, coming forward up the room, "stop a bit. I tell you what, Mr Mell, once for all. When you take the liberty of calling me mean or base, or anything of that sort, you are an impudent beggar. You are always a beggar, you know; but when you do that, you are an impudent beggar."

Suddenly the whole school looked as if they had been turned into stone; and there was Mr Creakle in the midst of them, with Tungay at his side, and Mrs and Miss Creakle looking in at the door, as if they were frightened. Mr Mell, with his elbows on his desk, and his face in his hands, sat, for some minutes, quite still.

"Mr Mell," said Mr Creakle, shaking him by the arm; "you have not forgotten yourself, I hope."

"No, sir, no," returned the master, showing his face, and rubbing his hands in his great agitation. "No, sir, no. I have remembered myself. I could wish you had remembered me a little sooner, Mr Creakle. It—it would have been more kind, sir, more just, sir. It would have saved me something, sir."

Mr Creakle, looking hard at him, put his hand on Tungay's shoulder, and got his feet upon the form close by, and sat upon the desk; and, turning to

Steerforth, said: "Now, sir, as he don't condescend to tell me, what *is* this?"

Steerforth evaded the question for a little while, and said at length, "What did he mean by talking of favourites, then?"

"Favourites?" repeated Mr Creakle, with the veins in his forehead swelling quickly, "who talked about favourites?"

"He did," said Steerforth.

"And pray, what did you mean by that, sir?" demanded Mr Creakle, turning angrily on his assistant.

"I meant, Mr Creakle," he returned in a low voice, "as I said; that no pupil had a right to avail himself of his position of favouritism to degrade me."

"To degrade *you*? My stars! But give me leave to ask you, Mr What's-your-name, whether when you talk of favouritism you show proper respect to me? To me, sir, the principal of the establishment, and your employer?"

"It was not judicious, sir, I am willing to admit," said Mr Mell. "I should not have done so, if I had been cool."

Here Steerforth struck in.

"Then he said I was mean, and then he said I was base, and then I called him a beggar. If *I* had been cool, perhaps I should not have called him a beggar. But I did, and I am ready to take the consequences of it."

"'I am surprised, Steerforth—although your candour does you honour," said Mr Creakle, "does you honour, certainly—I am surprised, Steerforth, I must say, that you should attach such an epithet to any person employed and paid in Salem House, sir."

Steerforth gave a short laugh.

"That's not an answer, sir," said Mr Creakle, "to my remark."

"Let him deny it," said Steerforth.

"Deny that he is a beggar, Steerforth?" cried Mr Creakle, "why, where does he go a-begging?"

"If he's not a beggar himself, his near relation's one. It's all the same."

Steerforth glanced at David, and Mr Mell's hand patted David gently upon the shoulder. David looked up with a flush upon his face and remorse in his heart; but Mr Mell's eyes were fixed on Steerforth.

"Since you expect me, Mr Creakle, to justify myself," said Steerforth, "and to say what I mean—what I have to say is, that his mother lives on charity in an almshouse."

Mr Mell still looked at him, and still patted David kindly on the shoulder, and said to himself in a whisper, "Yes, I thought so."

Mr Creakle turned to his assistant with a severe frown: "Now you hear what this gentleman says, Mr Mell. Have the goodness, if you please, to set him right before the whole school."

"He is right, without correction," returned Mr Mell, in the midst of a dead silence; "what he has said is true."

"Be so good as to declare publicly," said Mr Creakle, "whether it ever came to my knowledge until this moment."

"I apprehend you never supposed my worldly circumstances to be very good,' said Mr Mell; "you know what my position is, and always has been here."

"I apprehend, if you come to that," said Mr Creakle, with his veins swelling again bigger than ever, "that you've been in a wrong position altogether, and mistook this for a charity school. Mr Mell, we'll part, if you please. The sooner the better."

"There is no time," said Mr Mell, rising, "like the present."

"Sir, to you!" said Mr Creakle.

"I take my leave of you, Mr Creakle, and all of you," said Mr Mell, glancing round the room, and again patting David on the shoulder. "James Steerforth, the best wish I can leave you is that you may come to be ashamed of what you have done today. At present I would rather see you anything than a friend, to me, or to anyone I feel an interest in."

Once more he laid his hand on David's shoulder; and taking his flute and a few books from his desk, and leaving the key in it for his successor, he went out of the school with his property under his arm.

Mr Creakle, who was inclined to cringe to Steerforth on account of his position and wealth, then made a speech thanking Steerforth for upholding the respectability of Salem House, and told the boys to give three cheers for him.

Mr Creakle then caned Tommy Traddles for crying at Mr Mell's departure, instead of cheering for Steerforth; and went back to his bed on his sofa, or wherever he had come from.

The boys were left to themselves, and looked blankly at each other. David could have cried, but that he feared it would offend Steerforth. Steerforth was very angry with Traddles, and said he was glad he had caught it.

Traddles said he didn't care. Mr Mell was ill-used.

"Who has ill-used him, you girl?" said Steerforth, feeling a little ashamed, but much too proud to own it.

"Why, you have."

"What have I done?" said Steerforth.

"Whatever have you done?" retorted Traddles. "Hurt his feelings, and lost him his situation."

"His feelings will soon get the better of it, I'll be bound," said Steerforth. "His feelings are not like yours, Miss Traddles. As to his situation—which was a precious one, wasn't it?—do you suppose I am not going to write home, and take care that he gets some money, Polly?"

The boys thought this very noble of Steerforth, whose mother was a rich widow, and would do almost anything for her son, it was said, that he asked her.

But that night David thought of the old flute, and wondered whether Mr Mell was playing sorrowfully somewhere, and felt very wretched indeed.

The new master came from a grammar school; and Steerforth declared him to be a brick; but he never took the pains with David that Mr Mell did.

8

Visitors for David

One afternoon, when Mr Creakle was laying about him dreadfully, Tungay came in, and called out, "Visitors for Copperfield!"

David stood up, quite faint with astonishment, and was told to go by the back stairs to get a clean frill on before going into the dining-room.

He wondered whether it was his mother, and went to the door quite in a flutter, and had to stop a sob before he went in.

It was Mr Peggotty and Ham.

They stood ducking at him with their hats, and squeezing one another against the wall. David laughed at the pleasure of seeing them again, and they all shook hands very cordially; but tears were very near the laughter too, and David, though he still laughed, pulled his handkerchief out and wiped his eyes; he was so much overcome at the sight of them.

Mr Peggotty nudged Ham to say something.

So Ham began, "Cheer up, Mas'r Davy bor'! Why, how you have growed!"

"Am I grown?" said David.

"Growed, Mas'r Davy bor'? Ain't he growed!" said Ham.

"Ain't he growed!" said Mr Peggotty.

"Do you know how mamma is, Mr Peggotty? And how my dear, dear old Peggotty is?"

"Oncommon," said Mr Peggotty.

"And little Em'ly, and Mrs Gummidge?"

"On—common," said Mr Peggotty.

There was a silence. Mr Peggotty, to relieve it, took two prodigious lobsters, and an enormous crab, and a large canvas bag of shrimps out of his pockets, and piled them up in Ham's arms.

"You see," said Mr Peggotty, "knowing as you was partial to a little relish with your wittles when you was along with us, we took the liberty. The old mawther biled 'em. Yes," said Mr Peggotty, because he had nothing else to say just then, "Mrs Gummidge, I do assure you, she biled 'em."

David thanked him heartily.

"We come, you see," said Mr Peggotty, "the wind and tide making in our favour, in one of our Yarmouth lugs to Gravesen'. My sister she wrote to me the name of this here place, and wrote to me as if ever I chanced to come to Gravesen', I was to come over and inquire for Mas'r Davy, and give her dooty, humbly wishing him well, and reporting of the fam'ly as they was oncommon toe-be-sure. Little Em'ly, you see, she'll write to my sister when I go back, as I see you, and as you was similarly oncommon, and so we make it quite a merry-go-rounder."

David thanked him again, and asked if little Em'ly was altered.

"She's getting to be a woman, that's wot she's getting to be," said Mr Peggotty. "Ask him."

He meant Ham, who beamed with delight and assent over the bag of shrimps.

"Her pretty face!" said Mr Peggotty, with his own shining like a light.

"Her learning!" said Ham.

"Her writing!" said Mr Peggotty. "Why it's as black as jet. And so large it is, you might see it anywheres."

He was going to say more about his little favourite, when Steerforth suddenly looked in, and, stopping in a song he was singing, said: "I didn't know you were here, young Copperfield!" (for it was not the usual visiting-room) and crossed by on his way out.

David, partly to show off his fine friend, Steerforth, and partly to explain to Steerforth how he came to have such visitors as these rough boatmen, called out, "Don't go, Steerforth, if you please. These are two Yarmouth boatmen—very kind, good people—who are relations of my nurse, and have come from Gravesend to see me."

"Ay, ay," said Steerforth, returning. "I am glad to see them. How are you both?"

There was an ease in his manner—a gay and light manner it was, but not swaggering, added to his delightful voice, his handsome face and figure, which seemed to carry a spell with him, and which not many persons could withstand. Mr Peggotty and Ham were at home with him at once. David told them in a few words how kind Steerforth was to him.

"Nonsense!" said Steerforth, laughing.

"And if Mr Steerforth ever comes into Norfolk or Suffolk, Mr Peggotty," said David, "while I am there, you may depend upon it I shall bring him to Yarmouth, if he will let me, to see your house. You never saw such a good house, Steerforth. It's made out of a boat!"

"Made out of a boat, is it?" said Steerforth. "It's the right sort of a house for such a thorough-built boatman!"

"So 'tis, sir, so 'tis, sir,' said Ham, grinning. "You're right, young gen'lm'n. Mas'r Davy, bor', gen'lm'n is right. A thorough-built boatman! Hor! hor! That's what he is too!"

And Mr Peggotty said, chuckling, and tucking in the ends of his neckerchief at his breast, "I thankee, sir, I thankee! I do my endeavours in my line of life, sir."

"The best of men can do no more, Mr Peggotty," said Steerforth, who had got his name already.

"I'll pound it's wot you do yourself, sir," said Peggotty, "and wot you do well—right well! I thankee, sir."

And Mr Peggotty wound up with an invitation to Steerforth to come and see him some day "along with Mas'r Davy," and wished them both well and happy.

Ham echoed his uncle's wish, and the boys parted with them in the heartiest manner; and then carried the shell-fish up into the bedroom unobserved, where they made a great supper that evening.

Poor Traddles ate too much crab, and was taken ill in the night; so ill, that he had to be drugged with black draughts and blue pills; and got a caning next day, with six chapters of Greek Testament for refusing to confess what he had eaten to make him sick.

And so the first half-year of David's school life passed away, and holidays loomed nearer and nearer. He began to be afraid that Mr Murdstone would not let him go home for them; but his fear was turned to joy at last, and one glad day he found himself inside the Yarmouth mail, and going home.

The coach stopped at Yarmouth; but not at the old hotel where the waiter had helped him with his chops and pudding. The hotel was called the Dolphin, and David was shown up into a nice little bedroom for the night; and Barkis the carrier was to call for him in the morning.

Barkis received him as if he had parted with him only five minutes ago, and as soon as the box and David were in the cart, the lazy horse walked off at his accustomed pace.

"You look very well, Mr Barkis," said David. "I gave your message. I wrote to Peggotty."

"Ah!" said Mr Barkis. He seemed gruff, and answered drily.

"Wasn't it right, Mr Barkis?" asked David after a little hesitation.

"Why, no," said Barkis.

"Not the message?"

"The message was right enough, perhaps," said Barkis, "but it come to a end there."

"Come to an end, Mr Barkis?"

"Nothing come of it," Barkis explained, looking sideways at David. "No answer."

"There was an answer expected, was there, Mr Barkis?" asked David, opening his eyes.

"When a man says he's willin," said Barkis, "it's as much as to say that man's a waitin' for an answer."

"Well, Mr Barkis?"

"Well," said Barkis, looking at the horse's ears; "that man's been a-waitin' for a answer ever since."

"Have you told her so, Mr Barkis?"

"N—no," growled the carrier, reflecting "I ain't got no call to go and tell her so. I never said six words to her myself. *I* ain't goin' to tell her so."

"Would you like me to do it, Mr Barkis," said David doubtfully.

"You might tell her, if you would," said Barkis, "that Barkis was a waitin' for a answer. Says you—what name is it?"

"Her name?"

"Ah!" said Barkis with a nod of his head.

"Peggotty."

"Chrisen name? Or nat'ral name?"

"Oh! it's not her Christian name. Her Christian name is Clara."

"Is it, though?' said Barkis. He pondered a good while on this circumstance, and resumed at length. "Says you, 'Peggotty, Barkis is a-waitin' for a answer.' Says she, perhaps, 'Answer to what?' Says you, 'To what I told you.' 'What is that?' says she. 'Barkis is willin',' says you."

At that the carter gave David a nudge with his elbow in the side, and slouching over his horse as usual, made no other reference to the subject. But half an hour after, he took a piece of chalk from his pocket, and wrote up, inside the tilt of his cart, "Clara Peggotty."

And now the old house is in sight, where the tall elm trees swing their naked branches in the wintry air, and shreds of the old rooks' nests drift away upon the wind.

The carrier put his box down at the garden gate, and left him; and David walked along the old path, glancing up at the windows, and fearing at every step to see Mr or Miss Murdstone looking out of one of them.

9

Just like Old Times

He reached the door, and turned the handle without waiting to knock, and went in with a quiet, timid step. He heard a low voice singing in the parlour; it was his mother's voice; and the tune she sang sounded like an old song she used to sing when David was a baby.

He looked into the room. She didn't see him. She was sitting by the fire with a baby in her arms, whose tiny hand she held against her cheek. Her eyes were looking down upon its face. And there was nobody else in the room.

David spoke, and then she started, and seeing him, she called him her dear Davy, her own boy! And coming half across the room to meet him, kneeled down upon the ground and kissed him, and laid his head on her bosom, near the little creature that was nestling there, and put its hand up to his lips.

"He is your brother," she said, fondling David. "Davy, my pretty boy! My poor child!" Then she kissed him more and more, and clasped him round the neck, when Peggotty came running in, and bounced down on the ground beside them, and went mad about them for a quarter of an hour.

It was as if the dear old days were back again.

David had arrived earlier than they had expected, and Mr and Miss Murdstone were out upon a visit, and would not be home till night.

Oh! it was a happy time. They dined together by the fireside with Peggotty in attendance to wait on them; but the mother wouldn't let her do it, and made her sit down and eat her dinner with them. David had his old plate, with a man-of-war in full sail upon it, which Peggotty had hoarded away, and would not have had broken, she said, for a hundred pounds. There was his old mug with "David" on it, and his old little knife and fork that wouldn't cut.

And while they ate their dinner and were happy, David began to tell Peggotty about Mr Barkis, and before she had finished, she began to laugh, and threw her apron over her head.

"Peggotty!" said David's mother, "what's the matter?"

Peggotty only laughed the more, and held her apron tight over her face when the mother tried to pull it away.

"What are you doing, you stupid creature?" said David's mother, laughing too.

"Oh! drat the man!" cried Peggotty. "He wants to marry me."

"It would be a very good match for you, wouldn't it?" said David's mother.

"Oh! I don't know." said Peggotty. "Don't ask me. I wouldn't have him if he was made of gold. Nor I wouldn't have anybody."

"Then why don't you tell him so, you ridiculous thing?"

"Tell him so?" retorted Peggotty, looking out of her apron. "He has never said a word to me about it. He knows better. If he was to make so bold as say a word to me, I should slap his face!"

Her own face was very red, and every now and then she laughed heartily.

David, looking at his mother, saw that though she smiled when Peggotty looked at her, she became very serious and thoughtful. Her face was still pretty, but it looked careworn and delicate, and she looked at Peggotty in an anxious, fluttered way; and putting out her hand, and laying it affectionately on the hand of her old servant, she said, "Peggotty dear, you are not going to be married?"

"Me, ma'am? Lord bless you, no!"

"Not just yet," said the mother tenderly.

"Never," cried Peggotty.

"Don't leave me, Peggotty," she said, taking her hand. "Stay with me. It will not be for long, perhaps. What should I ever do without you?"

"Me leave you, my precious?" cried Peggotty. "Not for all the world and his wife. Why, what's put that into your silly little head?"

The mother didn't answer except to thank her, and Peggotty went on:

"Me leave you! I think I see myself. No, no, my dear! Peggotty go away from you? Not she, my dear. It isn't as there ain't's some Cats that would be well enough pleased if she did, but they shan't be pleased. They shall be aggravated. I'll stay with you till I'm a cross, cranky old woman. And when I'm too old to be of use to anyone, I shall go to my Davy, and ask him to take me in."

"And I shall be glad to see you," said David; "and I'll make you as welcome as a queen."

"Bless you! dear heart," said Peggotty kissing him. "I know you will." And then she took the baby out of its cradle and nursed it; and then she cleared the table, and then she came in with another cap, and her work-box, and they all sat round the fire and talked delightfully.

David told them what a hard master Mr Creakle was, and they pitied him very much. And he told them all about Steerforth, and Peggotty said she would walk a score of miles to see him. And when the baby was awake David took him in his arms and nursed him lovingly; and when it was asleep again, he crept up to his mother's side with his arm around her waist, and his cheek upon her shoulder, and felt once more her beautiful hair drooping over him just like an angel's wing.

It seemed as if he had never been away; and that there were no such persons as Mr and Miss Murdstone in the world.

It was a happy time, indeed.

"I wonder," said Peggotty suddenly, "what's become of Davy's great aunt?"

"What nonsense you talk, Peggotty," said David's mother, rousing herself from a reverie.

"Well, but I really do wonder, ma'am," said Peggotty.

"What can have put such a person into your head? Miss Betsey is shut up in her cottage by the sea, no doubt, and will remain there," said David's mother "At all events, she is not likely ever to trouble us again."

"No!" mused Peggotty. "No. That ain't likely at all—I wonder, if she was to die, whether she'd leave Davy anything?"

"Good gracious me, Peggotty! What a nonsensical woman you are! When you know that she took offence at the poor dear boy's ever being born at all!"

For you may remember how Miss Betsey marched out of the house when she heard that the baby was a boy, and never came back again.

By and by they had their tea, and the fire was made up and the candles snuffed; and David told them more about Salem House, and a good deal more about Steerforth; and it was nearly ten o'clock before they heard the sound of wheels.

They all got up then, and David's mother said hurriedly, that it was so late that David had perhaps better go to bed. So he kissed her and went upstairs with his candle directly, before the Murdstones came in; and as he climbed the stairs he fancied the Murdstones brought a blast of cold air into the house with them, which blew away the old familiar feeling.

David was uncomfortable about going down to breakfast next morning, as he had never set eyes on

Mr Murdstone since he had bitten him that never-to be-forgotten day.

But he had to go down, and found Mr Murdstone standing with his back to the fire, while Miss Murdstone made the tea.

Mr Murdstone looked at David as if he didn't know who he was; but the look was cold and steady.

David felt confused; but going up to him he said, "I beg your pardon, sir. I am very sorry for what I did, and I hope you will forgive me."

"I am glad you are sorry, David," he replied; and gave him the hand that David had bitten. He saw the scar upon it.

David grew very red, and said, "How do you do, ma'am?" to Miss Murdstone.

"Ah, dear me!" sighed Miss Murdstone, giving him the tea-caddy scoop to shake instead of her fingers. "How long are the holidays?"

"A month, ma'am."

"Counting from when?"

"From today, ma'am."

"Ah!" said Miss Murdstone. "Then there's one day off."

She was very angry when she saw David later on with the baby in his arms; she was sure he would let it fall; and told his mother he must never carry the baby again. And she was still more angry when the mother said that the baby's eyes were just like David's; and she stalked out of the room and banged the door.

The holidays, of course, were not very happy ones. How could they be with the Murdstones there? David felt that his mother was afraid to speak to him, or to be kind to him in their presence, lest she should give them offence somehow; so he used to steal into the kitchen to sit with Peggotty, where he never felt in the way.

But Mr Murdstone objected to that.

"I am sorry to observe," he said, "that you have an attachment to low and common company. You are not to associate with servants. The kitchen will not improve you."

Oh! the weary hours he passed in the parlour, day after day, afraid to move a leg or an arm lest Miss Murdstone should complain of his restlessness!

What walks he took alone, down muddy lanes in the bad winter weather to get away from their presence! What a relief it was to hear Miss Murdstone hail the first stroke of nine at night, and order him off to bed!

He was not sorry when the holidays were over; he was looking forward to seeing Steerforth again. He was not sorry when Barkis appeared at the gate and carried his boy into the cart.

He kissed his mother and his baby brother, and felt a little sorry then. She pressed him to her; but Miss Murdstone was there, and then she had to let him go.

But when he was in the cart and it was moving away, he heard her calling him. He looked out, and she was standing at the garden gate alone, holding up the baby in her arms for him to see.

It was cold, still weather; and not a hair of her head, or a fold of her dress, was stirred, as she looked intently at him, holding up the child.

David never saw her again.

10

A Memorable Birthday

He had been at school just two months when his birthday came round again. A fog hung about the place, and there was hoarfrost on the ground—a bitter, raw, cold March morning.

Breakfast was over and the boys had been called in from the playground when Mr Sharp entered the schoolroom and said, "David Copperfield is to go into the parlour."

David's heart gave a bound. He was expecting a birthday hamper from Peggotty. And the boys had told him not to forget them when the good things came, for they knew what he was looking forward for. He jumped up very readily.

"Don't hurry, David," said Mr Sharp, in an unusually soft tone. "There's time enough, my boy, don't hurry."

But David did hurry into the parlour, where Mr Creakle was sitting at breakfast with the cane and a newspaper before him. David didn't see the hamper.

"David Copperfield," said Mrs Creakle, taking him to a sofa, and sitting down beside him, "I want to speak to you very particularly. I have something to tell you, my child."

Mr Creakle shook his head, and stopped up a sigh with a very large piece of buttered toast.

"You are too young to know how the world changes every day," said Mrs Creakle, "and how the people in it pass away. But we all have to learn it, David; some of us when we are young, some of us when we are old, some of us at all times of our lives."

David looked at her earnestly.

"When you came away from home at the end of the vacation," said Mrs Creakle, after a pause, "were they all well?" And after another pause, "Was your mamma well?"

A mist seemed to arise between David and Mrs Creakle. He felt burning tears in his eyes.

"She is very dangerously ill," she said.

David knew what was coming.

"She is dead," said Mrs Creakle.

He gave out a desolate cry, and felt an orphan in the wide, wide world.

Mrs Creakle was very kind to him. She kept him in the parlour all day, and left him alone sometimes. He cried and wore himself to sleep, and awoke and cried again; and there was a dull weight on his breast; and he thought of her as he had seen her last—holding up the baby at the gate.

He thought of the house shut up and hushed; and of the little baby who Mrs Creakle said, had been pining away for some time, and who, they believed, would die too; and he thought about going home, for they had sent for him to attend the funeral.

He walked that afternoon in the playground while the other boys were in school; and they had no story-telling that night in the bedroom, and Traddles insisted on lending him his pillow, although he had one of his own.

He left Salem House the next afternoon; and left it never to return; but he did not know that then.

He looked out for Barkis's familiar face at Yarmouth; but a short, merry-looking little old man in black, came puffing up to the coach window and said, "Master Copperfield?"

"Yes, sir."

"Will you come with me, young sir, if you please," he said, opening the door; "and I shall have the pleasure of taking you home."

And David, wondering who he was, walked away with him to a shop, on which was written OMER, DRAPER, TAILOR, HABERDASHER, FUNERAL FURNISHER, etc.

Mr Omer had taken him there to have him measured for a suit of mourning, and after that he drove him to Blunderstone.

He was in Peggotty's arms before he got to the door, and she took him into the house. She cried very much, and spoke in whispers, and walked softly, as if the dead could be disturbed. The little baby was dead too, and they had put him in his mother's arms.

Mr Murdstone did not heed him when he went into the parlour, but sat over the fire with red eyes. Miss Murdstone gave him her finger nails to shake—she was very busy writing letters—and asked him in an iron whisper if he had been measured for his mourning.

She wrote all day, and seemed to take a pleasure in her firmness, and her strength of mind; and never relaxed a muscle of her face, nor softened a tone of her voice.

Mr Murdstone took a book sometimes to read, but would remain a whole hour without turning a leaf, and then would put it down, and walk restlessly to and fro.

In these days before the funeral David saw but little of Peggotty; but at night she always came to him and sat by his bed till he fell asleep.

And after the funeral—that sad day that David never forgot—she went with him up to his little room, and sat with him on his little bed, and, holding his hand, told him all there was to tell.

"She was never well," said Peggotty, "for a long while. I think she got to be more timid, and more frightened like of late; and that a hard word was like a blow to her. But she was always the same to me. She never changed to her foolish Peggotty, didn't my sweet girl. The last time that I saw her like her own old self was the night when you came home, my dear. The day you went away, she said to me, 'I shall never see my pretty darling again. Something tells me so, that tells me the truth, I know. God protect and keep my fatherless boy.'"

"I never left her afterwards," said Peggotty. "She

often talked to them two downstairs—for she loved them; she couldn't bear not to love anyone who was about her—but when they went away from her bedside, she always turned to me, as if there was rest where Peggotty was, and never fell asleep in any other way.

"On the last night, in the evening, she kissed me, and said, 'Let my dearest boy go with me to my resting place, and tell him that his mother, when she lay here, blessed him not once, but a thousand times. . . . Peggotty, my dear, put me nearer to you'; for she was very weak. 'Lay your good arm underneath my neck,' she said, 'and turn me to you, for your face is going far off, and I want it to be near.' I put it as she asked; and O Davy! the time had come when she was glad to lay her poor head on her stupid, cross old Peggotty's arm—and she died like a child that had gone to sleep!"

From that time David remembered her only as the young mother who had been used to wind her bright curls round and round her finger, and to dance with him at twilight in the parlour. In her death she winged her way back to her calm, untroubled youth, and cancelled all the rest.

11

Peggotty's Wedding

The first act of business that Miss Murdstone performed when the day of the funeral was over, was to give Peggotty a month's warning. As to David's future, not a word was said, nor a step taken. Once he mustered courage to ask Miss Murdstone when he was going back to school, and she answered drily that she believed he was not going back at all.

Neither of the Murdstones wanted him in the parlour, so he spent the time with Peggotty; and Mr Murdstone didn't seem to care as long as he didn't bother him.

"Davy," said Peggotty one day, "I have tried, my dear, all ways I could think of to get a suitable service here in Blunderstone, but there is no such thing, my love."

"And what do you mean to do, Peggotty?" he asked wistfully; for Peggotty was the only friend he had in the world now; and he clung to her.

"I expect I shall be forced to go to Yarmouth," replied Peggotty, "and live there."

"You might have gone further off," said David brightening, "and been as bad as lost. I shall see you sometimes, my dear old Peggotty, there. You won't be quite at the other end of the world, will you?"

"Contrary ways, please God!" cried Peggotty. "As long as you are here, my pet, I shall come over every week of my life to see you. One day every week of my life!"

And then she told him how she would go to her brother's first, till she had time to look about her for another situation. And then she said that, perhaps, as nobody seemed to want David there, they might let him go to Yarmouth with her for a while; and later on made so bold as to suggest this to Miss Murdstone.

"The boy will be idle there," said Miss Murdstone, looking into a pickle jar, "but to be sure he will be idle here—or anywhere, in my opinion." And after a while she added, "It is of paramount importance that my brother should not be disturbed or made uncomfortable. I suppose I had better say yes."

David thanked her, without making any show of joy, lest it should induce her to withdraw her consent. And when the month was out, Peggotty and he went away in the carrier's cart.

Peggotty was naturally in low spirits at leaving what had been her home for so many years. She had been walking in the churchyard too, very early, and she sat in the cart with her handkerchief at her eyes.

So long as she remained like this, Barkis gave no sign of life whatever; but when she began to look about her, he grinned at David several times.

"It's a beautiful day, Mr Barkis," remarked David.

"It ain't bad," said Mr Barkis.

"Peggotty is quite comfortable now, Mr Barkis."

"Is she, though?" said Mr Barkis.

After reflecting about it, Mr Barkis eyed her and said, "*Are* you pretty comfortable?"

Peggotty laughed and said yes.

"But really and truly, you know. Are you?" growled Mr Barkis, sliding nearer to her on the seat, and nudging her with his elbow. "Are you? Really and truly pretty comfortable? Are you? Eh?" and Mr Barkis nudged her again.

He was so polite as to stop at a public-house on their account, and entertain them with boiled mutton and beer, expressing his hope often that Peggotty was pretty comfortable.

Mr Peggotty and Ham were waiting for them at the old place, and shouldered the boxes and walked away, when Mr Barkis solemnly beckoned David with his forefinger.

"I say," growled Mr Barkis, "it was all right."

"Oh!" said David.

"It didn't come to an end there. It was all right."

"Oh!" said David again.

"You know who was willin'," said the carrier. "It was Barkis, and Barkis only." And he shook hands with David. "I'm a friend of your'n. You made it all right, first. It's all right."

David hadn't a notion as to what he meant; and stood staring at him till Peggotty called him away.

Then she asked him what Barkis had been saying to him, and David told her.

"Like his impudence," said Peggotty, "but I don't mind that. Davy dear, what should you think if I was to think of getting married?"

"Why—I suppose you would like me as much then as you do now," said David.

Peggotty hugged him in the road. "Tell me what you should say, darling?" she asked as they went along.

"If you were thinking of being married—to Mr Barkis, Peggotty?"

"Yes," said Peggotty.

"I should think it would be a very good thing. For then you know, Peggotty, you would always have the horse and cart to bring you over to see me, and could come for nothing, and be sure of coming."

"The sense of the dear!" cried Peggotty. "What I've been thinking of this month back!" And she added that she was unfit, perhaps, to go as a servant to a stranger; and talked of liking to have a home of her own, and being not far from her darling girl's resting-place.

"Barkis is a good plain creetur," said Peggotty, "and if I tried to do my duty by him, I think it would be my fault if I wasn't—if I wasn't pretty comfortable," and Peggotty laughed heartily.

David laughed too; and they talked of Mr Barkis till the boat-house came in sight.

Mrs Gummidge was waiting at the door, and everything was just the same in the dear old boat-house, down to the seaweed in the blue mug in the bedroom. But there was no little Em'ly to be seen, and David asked Mr Peggotty where she was.

"She's at school, sir," said Mr Peggotty; "she'll be home," looking at the Dutch clock, "in from twenty minutes to half an hour's time. We all on us feel the loss of her, bless ye."

Mrs Gummidge moaned.

"Cheer up, mawther," said Mr Peggotty.

"I feel it more than anybody else," said Mrs Gummidge. "I'm a lone lorn creetur, and she used to be a'most the only thing that didn't go contrairy with me."

Mr Peggotty shaded his mouth with his hand and whispered, "The old 'un!"

And David came to the conclusion that her spirits must be as low as ever.

By and by a little figure appeared in the distance. It was little Em'ly, and David went to meet her. She had grown taller, and looked so very pretty that David suddenly felt shy, and let her pass as if he didn't recognise her.

Little Em'ly only laughed and ran past him, and then David had to run after her to catch her up.

"Oh, it's you, is it?" said little Em'ly.

"Why, you knew who it was, Em'ly?" said David.

"And didn't *you* know who it was?" said Em'ly.

David was going to kiss her; but she said she wasn't a baby now, and ran away into the house.

"A little puss it is," said Mr Peggotty, patting her with his great hand.

"So sh' is! So sh' is!' cried Ham. "Mas'r Davy bor', so sh' is."

Little Em'ly was spoiled by them all; especially by Mr Peggotty, whom she could have coaxed into anything by only going and laying her cheek against his rough whiskers.

But she was very tenderhearted; and when they all sat round the fire after tea; and Mr Peggotty spoke very softly to David of his loss, the tears stood in little Em'ly's eyes.

"Ah!" said Mr Peggotty, taking up her curls, "here's another orphan, you see, sir. And here," said Mr Peggotty, giving Ham a backhanded knock in the chest, "is another of 'em, though he don't look much like it."

"If I had you for my guardian, Mr Peggotty," David answered. "I don't think I should feel much like it."

"Well said, Mas'r Davy bor!" cried Ham in an ecstasy. "Hoorah! Well said! Nor more you wouldn't I Hor! hor!" and Ham returned Mr Peggotty's backhander, and little Em'ly got up and kissed her uncle.

"And how's your friend, sir?" asked Mr Peggotty of David.

"Steerforth?" said David.

"That's the name!" cried Mr Peggotty, turning to Ham. "I knowed it was something in our way."

"You said it was Rudderford," observed Ham, laughing.

"Well," retorted Mr Peggotty, "and ye steer with a rudder, don't ye? It ain't far off. How is he, sir?"

David said he was very well when he last saw him, and launched out as usual in Steerforth's praise.

Mr Peggotty and Ham agreed to all he said, and little Em'ly listened with the deepest attention, her breath held, and her blue eyes sparkling like jewels.

The days passed pretty much as they had passed before, except that little Em'ly had more tasks to learn, and needlework to do, so that she could not walk so often with David on the beach.

Mr Barkis used to come to see them every evening. The first time, he brought a bundle of oranges tied up in a handkerchief for Peggotty; and the next day a double set of pigs' trotters, and another time a leg of pickled pork; and sometimes he took Peggotty out for a walk on the beach.

At last, just before David left them all, Mr Barkis drove up one morning in a chaise, dressed up very smartly in a new blue coat, to take Peggotty out for a holiday. David and little Em'ly were to go with them, and when they were seated in the chaise, Mr Peggotty offered Mrs Gummidge an old shoe to throw after them for luck.

"It had better be done by somebody else, Dan'l," said Mrs Gummidge. "I'm a lone lorn creetur myself, and everything that reminds me of creeturs that ain't lone and lorn goes contrairy with me."

"Come, old gal, take and heave it," said Mr Peggotty.

But Mrs Gummidge wouldn't; and Peggotty declared that she should; so Mrs Gummidge threw the shoe after them for luck, and burst into tears immediately, declaring that "she knowed she was a burden," and had better be carried to the workhouse at once.

David thought it was a very sensible idea, and wondered why they didn't do it.

Away they drove for their holiday excursion; and the first thing they did was to stop at a church, where Mr Barkis tied the horse to some rails, and went in with Peggotty, leaving the children outside.

They were a good while in the church, but came out at last, and then they drove away into the country.

"What name was it as I wrote up in the cart?" asked Mr Barkis of David with a wink.

"Clara Peggotty," said David.

"What name would it be as I should write up now if there was a tilt here?" said Mr Barkis.

"Clara Peggotty, again," suggested David.

"Clara Peggotty Barkis," answered the carrier, and burst into a roar of laughter.

So they were married, and had gone into the church for that purpose; and Peggotty had resolved to have a quiet wedding, because she wore her mourning dress still for her "dearest girl."

She gave David a very loving kiss to let him see that she loved him as much as ever; and the little party drove over to a little inn where they had a splendid dinner, and after that a very good tea. It was dark when they got into the chaise again, and they drove cosily back, looking up at the stars and talking about them.

Well, they came to the old boat-house again in good time at night; and there Mr and Mrs Barkis bade them goodbye and drove away snugly to their own home. David felt then, for the first time, that he had lost Peggotty; but Mr Peggotty and Ham, knowing what was in his mind, were ready with some supper, and their hospitable faces, to drive it away.

It was a night tide; and soon after they went to bed, Mr Peggotty and Ham went out to fish. David felt very brave at being left in the solitary house to protect little Em'ly and Mrs Gummidge, and only wished that a lion or a serpent would make an attack on them that he might destroy him, and cover himself with glory. But as nothing of the sort happened to be walking about on Yarmouth flats that night, David dreamed of dragons instead.

Peggotty came next morning, and after breakfast David took leave of Mr Peggotty, Ham, and Mrs Gummidge, and little Em'ly, and went back with Peggotty to her own home—and a beautiful little home it was.

That night David slept in a little room in the roof which was to be always his, Peggotty said, and should be kept for him in exactly the same state.

"Young or old, Davy dear, as long as I am alive and have this house over my head," said Peggotty, "you shall find it as if I expected you here every minute. I shall keep it every day as I used to keep your old little room, my darling; and if you was to go to China, you might think of it as being kept just the same, all the

time you were away." She said it with her arms round
his neck; and David needed no one to tell him how
true and constant she would be.

He tried to thank her, and tried not to cry; but his
heart was heavy, for in the morning he was going
home—home to Blunderstone and the Murdstones
again, and there would be no mother there, and no
Peggotty ever again.

Barkis drove them over in the carrier's cart next
morning, and they left him at the gate. And it was
strange to him to see the cart go on, taking Peggotty
away, and leaving him under the old elm trees looking
at the house in which there was no face to look on his
with love or liking, any more.

12

He goes out into the World

The Murdstones disliked him. They sullenly, sternly, steadily overlooked the boy. They were not actually cruel to him; they just neglected him. No one talked of school, and David hung about with nothing to do. He would rather have been sent to the hardest school that ever was kept, than go in this friendless, listless way; but at this time Mr Murdstone's business—he had something to do with a wine-merchant's house in London—was not prospering well, and he made that an excuse for not sending David to school; indeed, he tried to believe that the boy had no claim on him at all.

The Murdstones objected to his making friends in Blunderstone; and what was worst of all, they seldom allowed him to visit Peggotty. Perhaps they were afraid that the boy might complain of their treatment; but Peggotty, faithful to her promise, either came to see him, or met him somewhere near, once every week, and never came without some dainty of her own making.

Week after week, month after month, he lived this solitary life; when one day, loitering somewhere in his usual listless way, he came suddenly upon Mr Murdstone walking with a gentleman.

The gentleman laughed and spoke to David, and David looking at him felt he had seen him before, and then remembered that he was Mr Quinion, the gentleman he had seen at the hotel at Lowestout, when Mr Murdstone took him before him on his horse, to spend that day with his friends.

"And how do you get on, and where are you being educated?" asked Mr Quinion.

David didn't know what to reply, and glanced at Mr Murdstone.

"He is at home at present," said Mr Murdstone. "He is not being educated anywhere. I don't know what to do with him. He is a difficult subject"; and his eye darkened with a frown.

"Humph!" said Mr Quinion, looking at them both. "fine weather." And after a little while he added, "I suppose you are a pretty sharp fellow still?"

"Ay. He's sharp enough," said Mr Murdstone. "You had better let him go."

Mr Quinion took his hand off David's shoulder, and David hurried home: but, turning back, he saw them looking after him and talking, and he felt they were speaking of him.

Mr Quinion came to sleep at their house that night, and the next morning, after breakfast, as David was leaving the room, Mr Murdstone called him back.

"David," said he, "to the young, this is a world for action; not for moping and droning in—"

"As you do," added Miss Murdstone.

Mr Quinion looked out of the window.

"I suppose you know, David," went on Mr Murdstone, "that I am not rich. You have received some considerable education already. What is before you, is a fight with the world; and the sooner you begin it the better. You have heard the counting-house mentioned sometimes?"

"The counting-house, sir?" repeated David.

"Of Murdstone and Grinby, in the wine trade," he replied.

"I think I have heard the business mentioned, sir," said David vaguely.

"Mr Quinion manages that business," said Mr Murdstone, and suggests that it gives employment to some other boys, and that he sees no reason why it shouldn't, on the same terms, give employment to you."

"He having," put in Mr Quinion in a low voice, and half turning round, "no other prospect, Murdstone."

Mr Murdstone made an angry, impatient gesture and went on—"Those terms are, that you will earn enough yourself to provide for your eating and drinking, and pocket-money. Your lodging (which I have arranged for) will be paid by me. So will your washing—"

"Which will be kept down to my estimate," said Miss Murdstone.

"So you are now going to London, David, with Mr Quinion, to begin the world on your own account."

"In short, you are provided for," said Miss Murdstone, "and will please to do your duty."

David hardly knew whether he was pleased or frightened. He was barely ten years old, and to have to begin the world on his own account at that early age was naturally rather appalling.

But he hadn't much time to think about it, for the very next morning his small trunk was packed, and he found himself sitting in the postchaise that was carrying Mr Quinion to the London coach at Yarmouth—"a lone lorn creetur," indeed, as Mrs Gummidge might have said.

Murdstone and Grinby's warehouse was at the waterside, down by Blackfriars. It was a crazy old house with a wharf of its own, with old grey rats swarming in the cellars. David could hear them squeaking as they scuffled and grubbed about, when he went for the first time to the warehouse, with his trembling hand in Mr Quinion's.

Here he was handed over to the care of a lad with a ragged apron and a paper cap, called Mick Walker, who was summoned to show David his work.

It was to rinse and wash the bottles that were to be filled with wine, to hold them up against the light, and reject those that were cracked or flawed. There were corks to be fitted to them, or seals to be put up on the corks, and labels to be pasted on them when the bottles were filled with wine, which had then to be packed in casks.

Mick Walker told him that his father was a bargeman; and that the other boy who was to work with them was called Mealy Potatoes—a nickname that the warehousemen had given him on account of his mealy complexion.

Mealy's father was a waterman, and a fireman too, he said; and Mealy's little sister did imps in the Pantomimes, of which they seemed very proud.

David thought of Steerforth and Traddles, and the rest of the Salem House boys; and whenever Mick went out of the room to fetch anything, the tears rolled down David's cheeks, and mingled with the water in which he was washing the bottles, and he sobbed as if his heart would break.

At half-past twelve the boys got up to go to their dinner, and Mr Quinion tapped at the counting-house window, and beckoned to him to go into his room where he sat behind a desk.

David went in and saw there a stoutish, middle-aged man, in a brown surtout and black tights and shoes, with no more hair upon his head (which was a large one and very shining) than there is upon an egg. His clothes were shabby, but he had an imposing shirt collar on; and he carried a jaunty sort of stick, with a large pair of rusty tassels to it; and a quizzing-glass hung outside his coat.

"This is he," said Mr Quinion, meaning David.

"This," said the stranger, with a condescending roll in his voice, "is Master Copperfield. I hope I see you well, sir?"

David, who felt very ill at ease, said he was well, and hoped the gentleman was well also.

"I am," said the stranger, "thank Heaven, quite

well"; and he added that he had had a letter from Mr Murdstone asking him to receive David into his house.

"This is Mr Micawber," said Mr Quinion. "He has been written to by Mr Murdstone on the subject of your lodgings, and he will receive you as a lodger."

"My address," said Mr Micawber, "is Windsor Terrace, City Road. I—in short," said Mr Micawber with a genteel air— "I live there." David bowed.

"Under the impression," said Mr Micawber, "that your peregrinations in this metropolis have not as yet been extensive, and that you might have some difficulty in penetrating the arcana of the modern Babylon in the direction of the City Road—in short," said Mr Micawber, in a burst of confidence, "that you might lose yourself, I shall be happy to call this evening, and install you in the knowledge of the nearest way."

David thought it very friendly of him to take so much trouble, and thanked him with all his heart.

"At what hour," said he, "shall I—"

"At about eight," said Mr Quinion.

"At about eight," said Mr Micawber. "I beg to wish you good day." Then he put on his hat, and went out with his cane under his arm; very upright, and humming a tune when he was clear of the counting house.

Mr Quinion then told David that he was to make himself as useful as he could in the warehouse, and that his salary would be six shillings a week; and he put down the first week's salary there and then.

Mealy Potatoes undertook to carry his trunk to Mr

Micawber's, as it was too heavy for David to carry himself, and David gave him sixpence for his trouble out of his first week's salary; and then went out to a cook-shop near, and bought a meat-pie for another sixpence, and had a drink at a neighbouring pump.

At eight o'clock in the evening Mr Micawber appeared, and they walked away together, his new friend impressing the names of the streets, and the shapes of the corner houses upon him, as they went along, that he might find his way back easily in the morning.

The house in Windsor Terrace was shabby like its master; and like him, too, made all the show it could. He presented David to Mrs Micawber, a thin, faded lady, who was sitting in the parlour, nursing a baby, which was one of twins.

There were two other children beside the twins; Master Micawber aged four, and Miss Micawber aged three. There was also a dark-complexioned young woman, with a habit of snorting, who was servant to the family, and who told David, when he'd been there half an hour, that she was "a orfling," and came from St Luke's workhouse.

Mrs Micawber took him to his room, which was at the top of the house, and carried the babies with her. The room was rather close, and very scantily furnished.

"I never thought," said Mrs Micawber, "before I was married, when I lived with papa and mamma, that I should ever find it necessary to take a lodger.

But Mr Micawber being in difficulties, all considerations of private feeling must give way."

David said "Yes, ma'am."

"Mr Micawber's difficulties are almost overwhelming just at present," said Mrs Micawber; "and whether it is possible to bring him through them, I don't know."

Mrs Micawber told him, too, that she had tried to exert herself; and, indeed, the centre of the street door was perfectly covered with a great brass plate, on which was engraved, "Mrs Micawber's Boarding Establishment for Young Ladies"; but no young ladies had ever come to school there.

Indeed, the only visitors David ever saw there were creditors, who used to come at all hours; some of them were quite ferocious.

One dirty-faced man used to edge himself into the passage as early as seven o'clock in the morning, and call up the stairs to Mr Micawber, "Come! You ain't out yet, you know. Pay us, will you? Don't hide, you know; that's mean. I wouldn't be mean if I was you. Pay us, will you? You just pay us, d'ye hear? Come!" And sometimes he would go across the street and roar up "robbers" and "swindlers" at the windows where he knew Mr Micawber was.

It mortified Mr Micawber exceedingly. Sometimes he pretended he was going to cut his throat with his razor; but he would think better of it by and by, and after polishing up his shoes with extraordinary pains, would go out, humming a tune.

Mrs Micawber, too, would have a fainting fit at such times; but she would cheer up an hour later, send two teaspoons to the pawnbroker's, and with it pay for a meal of lamb chops, breaded, and a glass of warm ale.

Once, after the visit of a ferocious creditor, she fell under the grate in a swoon with a baby in her arms; but that same night she was able to eat a veal cutlet by the kitchen fire, and entertained David with stories of her papa and mamma, and the company they used to keep.

David passed all his leisure time with the Micawbers, and grew to like them very well. They provided him with only a bedroom. He bought all his food himself; and used to keep his bread and cheese in a little cupboard there to make his supper on when he came home at night.

All day long he washed the wine bottles with Mealy Potatoes and Mick Walker; but the secret agony of his soul was great when he remembered Traddles and Steerforth and thought of them growing up into re-fined and educated men, while his everyday companions were coarse and ignorant lads, and he himself had no hope of becoming anything better.

He felt degraded by his menial work, and felt, too, that he had done nothing to merit such degradation; and though he wrote to Peggotty often, he couldn't bring himself to let her know how miserably unhappy he was, partly for love of her, for it would have made *her* miserable, and partly because he was too much ashamed.

He never made a single acquaintance besides the Micawbers; nor spoke to any of the many boys whom he saw daily in going to and from the warehouse, and in prowling about the streets at meal-times. He grew more secret, and more self-reliant, and shabbier every day.

He never told the boys he worked with how he came to be there doing such menial work, nor let them know how much he hated it. He did his work and kept his counsel; but to think of Peggotty and his mother, and the dear old days, was to wellnigh break his heart.

The boys and men at the warehouse felt he was different from themselves. "The young gent" they grew to call him, and sometimes "the young Suffolker." Mealy Potatoes objected to this one day; but Mick Walker immediately put him down.

The foreman of the packers at the warehouse, a man named Gregory, and the carman, named Tipp, used to call him "David" sometimes; but that was generally after he had entertained them with bits out of *Roderick Random* and the rest of the dear old books.

He was so young and childish that sometimes he could not resist the stale pastry put out for sale at half price at the pastry cook doors, and spent his money in buying tartlets, and had to go without meat for his dinner.

Once he took his own bread with him wrapped in a piece of paper—he had brought it from home in the morning—and went into a fine, fashionable shop near Drury Lane, and ordered a small plate of beef to eat with his bread.

The waiter stared hard at the little fellow, but he brought him the beef, and then he called another waiter to come and look at him.

Oh! if his mother could have seen him now! Or Peggotty! Working from morning till night with common men and boys, a shabby child! Lounging about the streets at meal-times, insufficiently fed!

Nobody ever gave the boy advice; there was nobody to help or to encourage him. But for the mercy of God he might easily have become a little robber, or a little vagabond.

13

The Difficulties of the Micawbers

Mrs Micawber might have looked after him better, for she had really a kind heart; but she was so weighed down with her own cares and her difficulties to make both ends meet, and her anxieties about Mr Micawber's creditors, who became more ferocious every day, that she had no time to think of David as a little friendless child, who might be in need of a little motherly counsel now and then.

On the contrary, his going to and from the warehouse every day, on his own account, earning his living as if he were a man, made her look upon him as a youth of some experience, rather than a very small boy of ten; and she got into the habit of confiding to him her troubles, instead of trying to lighten his own.

David had a sympathetic nature, and was often more troubled about the Micawbers' troubles than the Micawbers were themselves; and used to walk about in his forlorn fashion, thinking of Mrs Micawber's ways and means, and heavy with the weight of Mr Micawber's debts.

Often on a Saturday night Mr Micawber would come home in floods of tears, declaring there was nothing before him but a jail; but after supper he would cheer up, and begin to calculate how much it would cost to put bow windows to the house "in case anything turned up," which was his favourite expression. And Mrs Micawber was just the same. In their kindness of heart they often invited the child to share their supper, but David always made some excuse, and would not accept the invitation—though he would have enjoyed it very much—because he knew they often had not too much for themselves.

And then his birthday came round again. His last birthday he had spent at Salem House—a memorable birthday, the day that Mrs Creakle sent for him to tell him that his mother was dead. How much had happened to him since then. He hardly felt that he was the same David Copperfield—"Young Copperfield" as Steerforth used to call him—spinning yarns in the bedroom at night, with Tommy Traddles laughing in the dark, and Steerforth refreshing him with sips of wine when he became a little "roopy."

David didn't tell anybody that it was his birthday, of course; he was too reserved for that; but he went to the bar of a public-house and asked the landlord—for it was a special occasion—"What is your best—your very best—ale, a glass?"

"Twopence halfpenny is the price of the Genuine Stunning Ale," said the landlord, staring at him.

"Then," said David, producing the money, "just draw me a glass of the Genuine Stunning, if you please, with a good head to it."

The landlord looked at him over the bar, from head to foot, with a strange smile on his face; and instead of drawing the beer, looked round the screen and said something to his wife.

She came out from behind it with her work in her hand, and stood beside her husband, looking at the strange small boy, with his old-fashioned face and manner.

They asked him what his name was, and how old he was, and where he lived, and how he was employed, and how he came there. David invented appropriate answers in his little mannish way. And then the landlord gave him the beer; but the landlord's wife, opening the little half-door of the bar, bent down and put his money back into his hand, and gave him a kiss that was half admiring and half compassionate, but all womanly and good.

The weeks and months went by. He wondered whether he would ever be rescued from this miserable existence; and thought hopelessly of growing up to be nothing more than a carman like Tipp, or a foreman packer like Gregory. He was forgetting what he had learned, too; and it made him unhappy, for in the old days David had been an ambitious boy, and was reckoned to be sharp and clever.

"Master Copperfield," said Mrs Micawber one day, meeting him with very red eyes, "I make no stranger of you, and therefore do not hesitate to say that Mr Micawber's difficulties are coming to a crisis."

It made David miserable to hear it—he had become quite fond of the Micawbers—he looked at her tearstained face with the utmost sympathy.

"With the exception of the heel of a Dutch cheese—which is not adapted to the wants of a young family," said Mrs Micawber, "there is really not a scrap of anything in the larder. I was accustomed to speak of the larder when I lived with papa and mamma, and I use the word almost unconsciously. What I mean to express, is, that there is nothing to eat in the house."

David was greatly concerned. He had two or three shillings in his pocket, as it was the middle of the week, and he pulled them out directly, and begged Mrs Micawber to take them as a loan, with tears in his own eyes.

But Mrs Micawber, making him put them back in his pocket, kissed him, and shook her head.

"No, my dear Master Copperfield, far be it from my thoughts. But you have a discretion beyond your years, and can render me another kind of service if you will; and a service I will thankfully accept."

David begged her to tell him what it was.

"I have parted with the plate myself," said Mrs Micawber. "Six tea, two salt, and a pair of sugars, I have at different times borrowed money on, in secret, with my own hands. But the twins are a great tie; and to me, with my recollections of papa and mamma, these transactions are very painful. There are still a few trifles that we could part with. Mr Micawber's feelings would never allow *him* to dispose of them; and Clickett"—this was the servant from the work-house—"being of a vulgar mind, would take painful liberties if so much confidence were reposed in her. Master Copperfield, if I might ask you—"

David guessed that she wanted *him* to sell some of the trifles she spoke of, and begged her to let him be of use. And the next morning, before he went to the warehouse, he took a few books to a bookstall in the City Road, and sold them for whatever they would bring.

After that he took something to sell or to pawn at the pawnbroker's every morning, before he went to his work.

The bookstall keeper used to get tipsy every night, and David would be ushered up to his bedroom, where he lay in a turn-up bed, with a cut in his forehead or a black eye, to bargain about the books; while his wife stood by, with her shoes down at heel, rating him soundly all the time.

Sometimes he couldn't find his money, and would ask David to call again; but his wife generally had some in her pocket, and would give David the money secretly as they went downstairs together.

He began to be well known at the pawnbroker's too; and the man behind the counter noticed him a good deal, and often got him to decline a Latin noun, or to conjugate a Latin verb for him while he transacted the business. Part of the money he brought home was always spent by Mrs Micawber on something extra nice for supper.

At last Mr Micawber's difficulties came to a crisis, and he was arrested early one morning, and taken to the King's Bench Prison. He told David, as they took him away, that the God of day had now gone down on him; and David, remembering when Roderick Random was in a debtors' prison, that there was a man there with nothing on him but an old rug, thought Mr Micawber's heart was broken as well as his own.

He spent a dismal day at the warehouse; but Mr Micawber cheered up in the prison, and played a lively game at skittles in the afternoon.

On the Sunday after, David was to go and have dinner with him (for the debtors' friends were allowed to visit them). Mr Micawber met him at the gate, and took him up to his little room, and solemnly conjured him to take warning by his fate; and said that "if a man had twenty pounds a year for his income, and spent nineteen pounds nineteen shillings and sixpence, he would be happy, but that if he spent twenty pounds one, he would be miserable."

Then he asked David to lend him a shilling, which he spent on a jug of porter, gave David a written order on Mrs Micawber for the amount, wiped his eyes, and put away his handkerchief.

They sat and talked before a little fire in a little rusty grate, till another debtor, who shared Mr Micawber's room, came in from the bakehouse with a loin of mutton on which the three made their dinner; and early in the afternoon, David returned home to let Mrs Micawber know how he had left her husband.

She fainted, in her agitation, when she saw David come in; and as soon as she had recovered, she made a little jug of egg-hot to comfort them while they talked over Mr Micawber's affairs.

Bit by bit the furniture was all sold; until at last Mrs Micawber resolved to move, with her children, into the prison, where Mr Micawber had now secured a room to himself; and David carried the key of the house to the landlord, who was very glad to get it.

David had become so used to the Micawbers that he didn't like to be parted from them; so a little room was hired for him outside the prison walls, and he used to take his breakfast with them every morning, and every evening he went to the prison, and walked up and down the parade with Mr Micawber.

The Micawbers lived more comfortably in the prison than they had lived out of it, for some relatives came to their assistance at this time, and helped them a good deal: and David, too, was now relieved of much of the weight of the family cares.

Mr Murdstone never inquired how David spent his time, and the boy never told any one at the warehouse. He still led the same secretly unhappy life, and his clothes were growing shabbier and shabbier.

Mr Murdstone never wrote to him. Miss Murdstone had on one or two occasions sent, through Mr Quinion, a parcel of mended clothes, with a scrap of paper enclosed in her handwriting to the effect that "J. M. trusted D. C. was applying himself to business, and devoting himself wholly to his duties." Nothing else! Not a word of anything else! The child might have become a little castaway for all they cared.

14

David makes a Resolve

And so the weeks and months went by in the same
dismal routine, until, through the help and advice of
Mrs Micawber's relations, Mr Micawber got his dis-
charge from the prison; and there was a prospect of
something turning up for Mr Micawber at last; but not
in London—away from London, and as David
walked home to his lodgings that evening, a weight
lay upon his heart at the thought of parting from his
only friends.

He could not sleep that night. He had grown to be so
accustomed to the Micawbers, and been so intimate
with them in their distress, and was so utterly friendless without them, that the prospect of going once
more among unknown people was misery to him.

He thought over all the shame and degradation of
the past year, and cried to himself that his life was
unendurable. Was there no hope of escape from it?
None. None at all—unless he himself ran away from
it!

To run away! The thought came to him as he lay
sleepless in bed, wondering what he would do after
the Micawbers had gone; and it gradually shaped itself into a settled resolution.

The Micawbers were going to Plymouth in a week's time, and during that time they took lodgings in the same house with David, and Mr Micawber went himself to the counting-house to tell Mr Quinion that he would have to relinquish his care of David on the day of his departure.

Mr Quinion called in Tipp, the carman, who was a married man, and had a room to let, and asked him if he could put David up. Tipp was only too glad, and David let them settle it so, and said nothing. *He* had made up his mind to run away as soon as the Micawbers had gone.

He never breathed a word about it to a soul, of course; and his reticence made him think the more. Where was he to go? A hundred times he asked himself that question, tossing sleeplessly on his bed; and a hundred times he went over that old story of his mother's about the day when he was born (a story she had loved to tell him, and which he had loved to hear) the story of Miss Betsey Trotwood—his father's aunt —marching into the house that windy March day, and bouncing out of it again, on hearing that the baby was a boy.

"Take off your cap, child, and let me see you—" he had heard the story so often—and how when his mother obeyed immediately, but with such nervous hands, her beautiful hair had fallen all about her face; and how Miss Betsey had cried, "Why bless my heart! You're a very baby!" in a very admiring voice.

He could not forget how his mother had thought

that she felt Miss Betsey touch her hair with no ungentle hand, and though it might have been his mother's fancy, David made a little picture out of the idea—the terrible aunt relenting towards the girlish beauty that he recollected so well, and forgiving her entirely for being a "wax doll."

If Miss Betsey knew of *his* sorrows, might she not forgive him for having been born a boy?

He did not even know where Miss Betsey lived; so he wrote a long letter to Peggotty, and asked her incidentally, if she remembered where it was; and asked her, too, if she could lend him half a guinea, which he wanted very particularly.

Peggotty's answer came immediately, with the half-guinea enclosed, a world of love, and with the information that Miss Betsey lived at Dover, but whether at Dover itself, at Hythe, Sandgate, or Folkestone, she could not say.

Then he asked one of the men at the warehouse if he could tell him where these last three places were, and the man telling him that they were all close together, David resolved to set out for Dover at the end of that very week.

He passed his evenings with Mr and Mrs Micawber, and they became fonder of one another as the time of their parting drew near. On the last Sunday they invited him to dinner; and they had a loin of pork, apple-sauce, and a pudding: and he gave his parting gifts to the children—a spotted horse which he had bought for little Wilkins Micawber, and a doll for little Emma.

They had a very pleasant day; but were sad about the coming separation.

"I shall never, Master Copperfield," said Mrs Micawber, "revert to the period when Mr Micawber was in difficulties, without thinking of you. Your conduct has been of the most delicate and obliging disposition. You have never been a lodger. You have been a friend."

"My dear," answered Mr Micawber, "Copperfield has a heart to feel for the distresses of his fellow creatures when they are behind a cloud, and a head to plan, and a hand—in short, a general ability to dispose of such available property as could be made away with."

He also begged David always to remember this piece of advice: "Annual income twenty pounds, annual expenditure nineteen nineteen six, result happiness. Annual income twenty pounds, annual expenditure twenty pounds ought and six, result misery."

David, very much affected, promised to keep these precepts in his mind; and the next morning he met the whole family at the coach office, and saw them, with a desolate heart, take their places outside, at the back.

"Master Copperfield," said Mrs Micawber, "God bless you! I never can forget all that you know, and I never would if I could."

"Copperfield," said Mr Micawber, "farewell! Every happiness and prosperity! In case of anything turning up (of which I am rather confident), I shall be extremely happy if it should be in my power to improve your prospects."

Mrs Micawber, sitting at the back of the coach with the children, and seeing David in the road looking wistfully up, suddenly seemed to wake up to the fact that he was only a very little boy, for she beckoned to him to climb up, and with a new and motherly expression in her face, she put her arm round his neck, and gave him just such a kiss as she might have given to her own boy.

David had barely time to get down again before the coach started, and he could hardly see the family for the handkerchiefs they waved.

It was gone in a minute; and David walked away to begin his weary day at Murdstone and Grinby's.

Being a very honest little fellow, and unwilling to disgrace the memory he was going to leave behind, he considered himself bound to remain until Saturday night; and as he had been paid a week's wages in advance when he first came there, he was not going to present himself in the counting-house to receive his salary. For this express reason he had borrowed the half-guinea, that he might have some money for his travelling expenses.

So when Saturday night came round, and they were all waiting in the warehouse to be paid, and Tipp, the carman, had gone in first to draw his money, David shook Mick Walker by the hand, and asked him to tell Mr Quinion that he had gone to move his box to

Tipp's; then he said a last goodbye to Mealy Potatoes, and then he ran away.

As he ran off to his lodging, he looked about for someone to help him to carry his box to the booking office for the Dover coach, and looked hard at a long-legged young man with an empty donkey cart in the Blackfriars Road.

"Well, sixpenn'orth of bad ha'pence," said the young man, "you'll know me agin to swear to."

David said he only looked at him because he thought he might like a job.

"Wot job?" said the long-legged young man.

"To move a box," said David.

"Wot box?"

David told him, and that it was in the next street, and that he'd give him sixpence to take it to the Dover coach-office.

"Done with you for a tanner," said the long-legged young man, and directly got upon his cart and rattled away at such a rate, that it was as much as David could do to keep pace with the donkey.

They went up to his little room and brought down the box together, and David asked him to stop for a minute when he came to the dead wall of the King's Bench Prison, where he wanted to put on a direction card; because he didn't want to put it on in the house, lest any of the landlord's family should see the direction, and guess what he was going to do.

The young man rattled on again, and David had

much difficulty in catching him up at the appointed place.

Being much flushed and excited, he tumbled his half-guinea out of his pocket in pulling out the card; and he put it into his mouth for safety, and with trembling hands had just tied the label to his box, when he felt himself violently chucked under the chin by the long-legged young man, and saw his half-guinea fly out of his mouth into the man's hand.

"Wot!" cried he, seizing David by the jacket collar, with a frightrul grin, "this is a pollis case, is it? You're going to bolt, are you? Come to the pollis, you young warmin, come to the pollis!"

"You give me my money back, if you please," said David, very much frightened; "and leave me alone."

"Come to the pollis!" repeated the young man, "you shall prove it yourn to the pollis."

"Give me my box and my money, will you?" cried David, bursting into tears.

The young man still replied, "Come to the pollis," with his hand on David's collar, when he changed his mind, jumped into the cart, sat upon the box, and exclaiming that he would drive to the pollis straight, rattled away harder than ever.

David ran after him as fast as he could, but he had no breath to call out. He was nearly run over twenty times at least in half a mile. Now he lost him, now he saw him, now he lost him again, now he fell down in the mud, now he ran into somebody's arms, now he went headlong at a post.

At length, confused by fright and heat, he couldn't run any more; and, panting and crying, but never stopping, he faced about for Greenwich, which he understood was on the Dover Road, with the wild idea of running, running on until he found his aunt.

15

His Eventful Journey

But his scattered senses came back to him when he had gone as far as the Kent Road; and sitting down on the doorstep of one of the terrace houses there, quite spent and exhausted, he wondered what he should do.

It was dark by this time, and the clocks were striking ten as he sat resting on the step; but it was a summer night fortunately, and fine weather.

In all his distress he had no notion of going back— he never dreamed of going back. As soon as he had recovered his breath he got up and went on.

He had just three-halfpence in his pocket, left out of his last week's wages; but he trudged on miserably, until he happened to pass a little shop where it was written up that ladies' and gentlemen's castoff clothes were bought. David's little experience with Mr and Mrs Micawber suggested to him that here might be a means of adding to his scanty store; so he went up the next side street, took off his waistcoat, rolled it neatly under his arm, and came back to the shop door, where the master was sitting in his shirtsleeves, smoking.

"If you please," said he, "I'm to sell this for a fair price."

Mr Dolloby—Dolloby was the name over the shop

door—took the waistcoat, stood his pipe on its head against the doorpost, went into the shop, followed by David, snuffed two candles with his fingers, spread the waistcoat on the counter, and looked at it there, held it up against the light, and looked at it there, and said:

"What do you call a price, now, for this here little weskit?"

"Oh! You know best, sir," returned David modestly.

"I can't be buyer and seller too," said Mr Dolloby. "Put a price on this here little weskit."

"Would eighteen pence be—" David hinted after some hesitation.

Mr Dolloby rolled it up again, and gave it back to him. "I should rob my family," he said, "if I was to offer nine pence for it."

David was disappointed, but there was no help for it. He said he would take nine pence for the waistcoat. And Mr Dolloby, not without some grumbling, produced nine pence. David wished him good night, and walked out of the shop with the money in his hand, and buttoned up his coat over his shirt.

On and on he trudged until he came to Blackheath —Blackheath, where his old school, Salem House, was,—and he thought he should like to sleep that night behind the wall at the back of the school, in a corner where there used to be a haystack. He imagined it would be a kind of company to have the boys, and the bedroom where he used to tell the stories, so near him.

He had had a hard day's work, and was pretty well

jaded when he found out Salem House. He walked round the old wall cautiously first, and looked up at the windows to see if all the lights were out. And then he found the corner with the haystack there, and lay down by it, for the first time in his life, without a roof above his head.

He slept soundly, for he was tired out, and dreamed of lying on his old school bed, talking to the boys in the room; and woke up with a start, crying out, "Steerforth! Steerforth!" and found himself sitting upright, looking wildly at the stars glistening and glimmering above him.

He felt afraid of he knew not what, the night was so lonely and silent, and he got up and walked about; but he was very weary, and soon lay down again, and slept till the ringing of the getting-up bell at Salem House awoke him.

He would have liked to have lurked about in the hope of seeing Steerforth come out, or even Traddles; but it was too risky, and he crept away as Mr Creakle's boys were getting up, and struck into the long dusty track which he had first known to be the Dover Road when he was one of them.

It was Sunday morning, and he heard the church bells ringing as he plodded on, and met the people who were going to church. He bought some bread, and still went on, and got that day through three and-twenty miles, passing many tramps on the road.

One or two little houses with the notice, "Lodgings for Travellers," hanging out, tempted him; but he was afraid of spending the few pence he had, and toiled on into Chatham, and crept at last upon a sort of grass-grown battery overhanging a lane, where a sentry was walking to and fro. Here he lay down near a cannon, happy in the society of the sentry's footsteps, and slept soundly till morning.

But he was stiff and sore of foot, and quite dazed by the beating of drums and marching of troops, and felt that he could not be able to go very far on his journey that day.

He had only a few pence left, and he thought the best thing he could do, before he left Chatham, was to sell his jacket. So he took it off and carried it under his arm—thankful that it was warm summertime—and began to look about for a likely shop.

There were lots of second-hand-clothes shops everywhere; but he wanted to find some little place like Mr Dolloby's; and at last took courage to enter a small low shop at the corner of a dirty lane. He had to go down two or three steps to go inside, and stepped down with a beating heart.

"Oh, what do you want?" cried an ugly old man, seizing David by the hair.

He was a dreadful old man to look at, in a filthy flannel waistcoat, and smelling terribly of rum. "Oh, my eyes and limbs, what do you want? Oh, my lungs and liver, what do you want? Oh, goroo, goroo!"

The last word was like a rattle in his throat.

"I wanted to know," said David trembling, "if you would buy a jacket?"

"Oh, let's see the jacket!" cried the old man. "Oh, my heart on fire, show the jacket to us! Oh, my eyes and limbs, bring the jacket out!"

With that he took his trembling hands, which were like the claws of a great bird, out of David's hair, and put on a pair of spectacles.

"Oh, how much for the jacket?" cried the old man, after examining it. "Oh, goroo!—how much for the jacket?"

"Half-a-crown," answered David, plucking up his courage.

"Oh, my lungs and liver!" cried the old man. "Oh, my eyes, no! Oh, my limbs, no! Eighteen pence. Goroo!"

He spoke in a sort of sing-song way ending in a high-pitched key, and every time he said "Goroo" his eyes seemed to be in danger of starting out.

"I'll take eighteen pence," faltered David, glad to have closed the bargain.

"Oh, my liver!" cried the old man, throwing the jacket on a shelf. "Get out of the shop! Oh, my lungs, get out of the shop! Oh, my eyes and limbs— goroo—don't ask for money; make it an exchange."

David was very much frightened; but he told him humbly that he wanted money, and that nothing else was of any use to him, but that he would wait for it, as he desired, outside, and had no wish to hurry him. So he went outside, and sat down in the shade in the corner.

By and by the boys in the streets came skirmishing about the shop, shouting out that the old man had sold himself to the devil, and bawled, "You ain't poor, you know, Charley, as you pretend. Bring out your gold. Come! It's in the lining of the mattress, Charley. Rip it open and let's have some."

Then they would offer him a knife for the purpose, and it exasperated him so much that he'd rush out of the shop after them, and send them flying.

All day long the boys teased him at intervals, and all day long he made frantic rushes after them.

He made many attempts to induce David to consent to an exchange, and came out with a fishing-rod one time, which David refused, beseeching him with tears to give him the money or the jacket; then he came out with a fiddle, and then with a cocked-hat, and then with a flute; but David refused them all, and sat on in desperation.

At last, to get rid of him, the old man began to pay him in halfpence, and was full two hours getting by easy stages to a shilling.

"Oh, my eyes and limbs!" he then cried, peeping hideously out of the shop, after a long pause, "will you go for twopence more?"

"I can't," said David, "I shall be starved."

"Oh, my lungs and liver, will you go for three pence?"

"I would go for nothing if I could," said David, "but I want the money badly."

"Oh, go—roo! Will you go for four pence?"

David was so faint and weary, for he had sat there all day, that he closed with this offer; and taking the money out of his claw, not without trembling, went away more hungry and thirsty than he had ever been before, and spent three pence on his tea; and feeling in better spirits after that, he limped seven miles upon his road, till he came to a little stream where he washed his aching feet, and then lay down under a haystack for the night.

His road the next morning lay through a succession of hop-grounds and orchards. Ripe apples hung on the trees, and the hop-pickers were busy at work. David thought it beautiful, and made up his mind to sleep among the hops that night. But the tramps he met on the road frightened him, for some of them looked at him quite ferociously.

One ruffian-looking fellow—a tinker—who had a woman with him, faced about and stared after the boy, and then roared out in such a tremendous voice to come back, that David halted and looked round.

"Come here, when you're called," said the tinker, "or I'll rip your young body open."

David felt it was best to go back, and as he went he noticed that the woman had a black eye.

"Where are you going?" said the tinker, gripping the bosom of his shirt with his blackened hand.

"I'm going to Dover."

"Where do you come from?" asked the tinker, giving his hand another turn in his shirt, to hold him more securely.

"I come from London," said David.

"What lay are you on? Are you a prig?"

"N—no," said David.

"If you make a brag of your honesty to me," said the tinker, "I'll knock your brains out. Have you got the price of a pint of beer about you? If you have, out with it, afore I take it away!"

David would have produced it at once, but that the woman slightly shook her head at him and formed, "No," with her lips.

"I am very poor," said David, "and have got no money."

"Why, what do you mean?" said the tinker, looking so sternly at him, that David almost feared he saw the money in his pocket.

"sir," stammered the boy.

"What do you mean," said the tinker, "by wearing my brother's silk handkercher? Give it over here!" And he had it off David's neck in a moment, and tossed it to the woman.

The woman burst into a fit of laughter, as if she thought this a joke, and tossed it back to David, nodded once, as slightly as before, and made the word "Go" with her lips.

But the tinker dragged the handkerchief out of the boy's hand, and putting it loosely round his own neck, turned upon the woman with an oath, and knocked her down.

This adventure frightened David so much that afterwards when he saw any of these people coming, he turned back till he found a hiding-place, where he remained till they had gone out of sight.

On, on he tramped, but, under all the difficulties of his journey, he was comforted and led on by the fanciful picture he had made of his stern aunt softening under the beauty of his fair young mother, and putting her hand tenderly on her pretty hair.

The picture was with him when he lay down to sleep among the hops; it was with him when he woke up in the morning; and it went before him all day.

16

How Miss Betsey Received Him

At last, on the sixth day after his flight, he set foot in the town of Dover; and then when he stood with his ragged shoes, and his dusty, sunburnt, half-clothed figure, the fanciful picture seemed to vanish like a dream, and he felt afraid and dispirited.

He asked some boatmen whom he met if they could tell him where Miss Trotwood lived. One said she lived in the South Foreland Light, and had singed her whiskers by doing so; another that she was made fast to the great buoy outside the harbour, and could only be visited at half-tide; and another that she was seen to mount a broom in the last high wind, and make direct for Calais.

Then he asked the fly-drivers, and they also made fun of him; and then he asked the shopkeepers, but they, without hearing what he had to say, replied that they had got nothing for him.

His money was all gone; and he could not spare any more clothes to sell. He was hungry, thirsty, and worn out, and more miserable and destitute than ever.

He sat down to rest on the step of an empty shop near the marketplace, when a fly-driver coming by with his carriage dropped his horsecloth. David handed it up, and something good-natured in the man's face encouraged him to ask if he could tell where Miss Trotwood lived.

"Trotwood," said he. "Let me see, I know the name, too. Old lady?"

"Yes, rather," said David.

"Pretty stiff in the back?"

David answered yes again.

"Carries a bag, is gruffish, and comes down upon you sharp?"

David's heart sank, for that is how Peggotty and his mother used to speak of her.

"I'll tell you what," said the man. "If you go up there," pointing with his whip toward the heights, "and keep right on till you come to some houses facing the sea, I think you'll hear of her. My opinion is, she won't stand anything, so here's a penny for you."

David accepted it thankfully, and bought a little loaf with it, and went on eating it, as he went where his friend directed him, till he came to the houses facing the sea. Then he went into a little shop close by, and asked the man behind the counter, who was weighing some rice for a young woman, if he could tell where Miss Trotwood lived.

"My mistress?" said the young woman quickly. "What do you want with her, boy?"

"I want to speak to her, if you please."

"To beg of her, you mean."

"No," said David, "indeed." And then he grew very red, and said nothing more.

The young woman put her rice in a little basket and walked out of the shop, telling David he could follow her if he wanted to know where Miss Trotwood lived.

David needed no second permission, and followed her till they came soon to a very neat little cottage with cheerful bow windows; in the front of it a small square gravelled court or garden full of flowers, carefully tended, and smelling deliciously.

"This is Miss Trotwood's," said the young woman. "Now you know, and that's all I have to say," and she hurried into the house, leaving David at the gate looking disconsolately over the top of it towards the parlour window, where a great chair made him imagine that his aunt might be seated at that moment in awful state.

His legs shook under him. His shoes were in a woeful condition. His hat was crushed and bent. His shirt and trousers, stained with heat, dew, and grass—and torn besides—might have frightened the birds from Miss Trotwood's garden, as he stood like a scarecrow at the gate. His hair had not been brushed or combed since he left London. His skin was burnt brown. From head to foot he was powdered white with dust. David trembled as he thought of introducing himself thus to his formidable aunt.

At one of the top windows he suddenly saw a florid, pleasant-looking gentleman, with a grey head, who winked at him, nodded his head, laughed and went away.

This strange behaviour so discomposed him that he

thought he would slink away; when there came out of the house a lady, with her handkerchief tied over her cap, and a pair of gardening gloves on her hands, wearing a gardening pocket like a tollman's apron, and carrying a great knife. David knew her immediately to be Miss Betsey, for she came stalking out of the house exactly as his mother had so often described her stalking up the garden at Blunderstone Rookery.

"Go away!" said Miss Betsey, shaking her head and making a distant chop in the air with her knife, "Go away! No boys here!"

He watched her with his heart in his mouth, as she marched to a corner of her garden, and stooped to dig up some little root there. Then David, in desperation, went softly in and stood beside her, and touched her with his finger.

"If you please, ma'am," he began.

She started and looked up.

"If you please, Aunt."

"EH?" exclaimed Miss Betsey in a tone of amazement.

"If you please, Aunt, I'm your nephew."

"Good gracious!" said Miss Betsey. And sat flat down in the garden path.

"I am David Copperfield, of Blunderstone, in Suffolk—where you came, on the night when I was born, and saw my dear mamma. I have been very unhappy since she died. I have been slighted, and taught nothing, and thrown upon myself, and put to work not fit for me. It made me run away to you. I was robbed at first setting out, and have walked all the way, and have never slept in a bed since I began the journey." Here he burst into a passion of crying, and cried as if his heart would break.

Miss Betsey gazed at him in wonder till he began to cry, when she got up in a hurry, collared him, and took him into the parlour, and unlocking a tall press, brought out several bottles and poured some of the contents of each in his mouth. Then she laid him, still sobbing, on the sofa, with a shawl under his head, and the handkerchief from her own head under his feet, lest he should dirty the cover; and then, sitting down, ejaculated at intervals, "Mercy on us!" letting off these exclamations like minute guns.

After a time she rang the bell; "Janet," said she to the young woman he had seen in the shop, "go up-stairs, give my compliments to Mr Dick, and say I wish to speak to him."

Janet stared in surprise at David lying stiffly on the sofa, but went on her errand, while Miss Betsey walked up and down the room until the gentleman who had squinted at him from the upper window came in laughing.

"Mr Dick," said she, "don't be a fool, because no-body can be more discreet than you can, when you choose. So don't be a fool, whatever you are."

The gentleman became serious immediately.

"Mr Dick," said Miss Betsey, "you have heard me mention David Copperfield? Now don't pretend not to have a memory, because I know better."

"David Copperfield?" said Mr Dick. "*David* Copperfield? Oh, yes, to be sure, David certainly."

"Well," said Miss Betsey, "this is his boy—his son. He would be as like his father as it's possible to be, if he was not so like his mother too."

"His son?" said Mr Dick. "David's son? Indeed."

"Yes," pursued Miss Trotwood, "and he has done a pretty piece of business. He has run away. And the question I put to you is, what shall I do with him?"

"Why, if I was you," said Mr Dick, considering, "I should"—looking at David's dusty figure—"I should wash him."

"Janet," said Miss Betsey, "Mr Dick sets us all right. Heat the bath."

Janet had gone away to get the bath ready, when Miss Betsey became suddenly rigid with indignation, and cried out, "Janet! Donkeys!"

Upon which Janet came running up the stairs as if the house were in flames, darted out on a little piece of green in front, and warned off two saddle donkeys, lady-ridden, that had presumed to set hoof upon it; while Miss Betsey, rushing out of the house, seized the bridle of a third donkey, carrying a child, led him off the green, and boxed the ears of the donkey-boy who had dared to bring them there.

Whether she had any lawful right-of-way over that patch of green, David never learned; but she had made up her mind that she had, and spent hours of her time in driving the donkeys off. There were three alarms before the bath was ready; and three times

Miss Betsey and Janet rushed out and drove the donkeys away.

The bath was a great comfort to David, for his bones were aching from lying out in the fields; and when he had bathed, Miss Betsey and Janet robed him in a shirt and a pair of trousers belonging to Mr Dick, and tied him up in two or three great shawls; gave him some broth to drink, and laid him on the sofa, where he soon fell asleep. And as he slept he seemed to dream that Miss Betsey came and bent over him, and put his hair from his face, and laid his head more comfortably, whispering, "Pretty fellow!" and "Poor fellow!" as she looked at him.

David awoke at last, and they then dined off a roast fowl and a pudding, David sitting at the table and looking like a trussed fowl himself, tied up in Mr Dick's trousers and shirt, and Miss Betsey's shawls.

He was deeply anxious to know what Miss Trotwood was going to do with him; but she ate her dinner in silence, only ejaculating "Mercy upon us!" when her eyes fell upon him.

Miss Betsey was a tall, hard-featured lady, but handsome too, although she looked so stern. Her eyes were very bright and her hair was grey, and she wore a lavender-coloured dress that was very neat, like everything else in the house.

Mr Dick's grey head was curiously bowed, and his large eyes looked vacantly about, as he rattled his money in his pockets, as if he were very proud of it. David thought he looked a little mad.

At last the cloth was removed, and some sherry put upon the table, of which David had a glass; and then Miss Betsey made him tell her all that had befallen him, asking him many questions, and bidding Mr Dick listen to his answers attentively.

"Whatever possessed that poor unfortunate Baby, that she must go and be married again," said Miss Betsey, when David had finished his story, "*I* can't conceive."

"Perhaps she fell in love with her second husband," suggested Mr Dick.

"Fell in love!" repeated Miss Betsey. "What do you mean? What business had she to do it?"

"Perhaps," simpered Mr Dick, after thinking a little, "she did it for pleasure."

"Pleasure, indeed!" said Miss Betsey. "She had had one husband. She had got a baby—oh, there were a pair of babies when she gave birth to this child sitting here! And what more did she want? And there's that woman with the Pagan name, that Peggotty—*she* goes and gets married next. Because she has not seen enough of the evil attending such things, *she* goes and gets married next, as this child relates. I only hope," said Miss Betsey, shaking her head, "that her husband is one of those poker husbands who abound in the newspapers, and will beat her well with one!"

David could not bear to hear his dear old Peggotty made the subject of such a wish, and told Miss Betsey how good, and true, and faithful, and devoted she was; that she loved him dearly, and that she had loved his mother dearly; and that he would have gone to her for shelter but for her humble station, which made him fear that he might bring some trouble on her; and David, thinking of Peggotty, broke down, and laid his face in his hands upon the table and cried.

"Well, well," said Miss Betsey, "the child is right to stand by those who have stood by him." She had her hand on his shoulder, and David, emboldened, was about to put his arms round her and beseech her protection, when Miss Betsey suddenly cried, "Janet! Donkeys!" and away she rushed with Janet at her heels, and the opportunity was gone for that moment, for she talked of nothing but her determination to bring actions for trespass against all the donkey proprietors of Dover, till teatime.

After tea they sat at the window till Janet brought in the candles and pulled down the blinds.

"Now, Mr Dick," said Miss Betsey, looking grave, "I am going to ask you another question. Look at this child! What would you do with him now?"

"Do with David's son?" said Mr Dick, looking at David with a puzzled face.

"Ay!" replied Miss Betsey, "with David's son."

"Oh," said Mr Dick. "Yes. Do with—I should put him to bed."

"Janet," said Miss Betsey triumphantly, "Mr Dick sets us all right. If the bed is ready, we'll take him up to it."

Janet said it was quite ready, and Miss Betsey led the way, with David following, and Janet in the rear.

Halfway up the stairs Miss Betsey stopped and asked what that smell of burning was; and Janet replied that she had been burning the ragged clothes that David had come in to the house.

The answer comforted David.

The room was a pleasant one, overlooking the sea, on which the moon was shining brilliantly.

He said his prayers and nestled into the snow-white sheets of the little white-curtained bed, and he thought of all the lonely places under the night sky where he had slept, and prayed again that he never might be houseless any more, and never might forget the houseless.

17

Miss Trotwood makes up Her Mind

Miss Betsey said nothing when he went down to breakfast next morning, but she looked so fixedly at him that David was overpowered with embarrassment.

In his confusion his knife tumbled over his fork, his fork tripped over his knife, he chipped bits of bacon a surprising height in the air, and choked himself with his tea, which persisted in going the wrong way instead of the right one, and sat blushing under Miss Betsey's close scrutiny.

"Hallo!" said she, after a long pause.

David looked up and met her sharp bright glance respectfully.

"I have written to him," said Miss Trotwood.

"To—?" David stammered.

"To your stepfather," said Miss Betsey. "I have sent him a letter that I'll trouble him to attend to, or he and I will fall out, I can tell him."

"Does he know where I am, Aunt?" asked David in alarm.

"I have told him," she answered with a nod.

"Shall I—be—given up to him?" faltered the child.

"I don't know," said Miss Betsey. "We shall see."

"Oh! I can't think what I shall do," cried David, "if I have to go back to Mr Murdstone!"

"I don't know anything about it," said Miss Betsey, shaking her head. "I can't say, I am sure. We shall see."

David's spirits sank under these words, and he became very downcast and heavy of heart.

His aunt took no notice of him, but went on with her daily occupations, and by and by brought out a workbox to her table, at the open window, and sat down to her work.

"I wish you would go upstairs," said Miss Betsey, as she threaded her needle, "and give my compliments to Mr Dick, and I'll be glad to know how he gets on with his Memorial."

David went upstairs, and found Mr Dick writing very fast with a quill pen, and his head almost laid on the paper. There was a quantity of ink in half-gallon jars on the table, and bundles of manuscript, and numbers of pens; and David also saw a large paper kite in the corner.

"Ha!" said Mr Dick, laying down his pen. "How goes the world? I'll tell you what, I shouldn't wish it to be mentioned, but it's a—" here he beckoned to David, and put his lips close to his ear—"it's a mad world. Mad as Bedlam, boy!" and Mr Dick took a pinch of snuff and laughed heartily.

David delivered Miss Betsey's message.

"Well," said Mr Dick, "my compliments to her, and I—I believe I have made a start. I think I have made a start." He put his hand among his grey hair, and asked, "You have been to school?"

"Yes, sir," answered David, "for a short time."

"Do you recollect the date," said Mr Dick, looking earnestly at him, "when King Charles the first had his head cut off?"

David said he thought it was in the year 1649.

"So the books say," said Mr Dick; "but I don't see how that can be. Because, if it was so long ago, how could the people about him have made that mistake of putting some of the trouble out of *his* head after it was taken off into *mine*?"

David couldn't tell him, and was very much surprised at the question. He was going away, when Mr Dick called his attention to the kite. "I made it," said Mr Dick. "We'll go and fly it, you and I."

"Well, child," said Miss Betsey, when he went downstairs, "and what of Mr Dick this morning?"

David said he sent his compliments, and was getting on very well indeed.

"What do you think of him?" said she.

After a little stammering, David said he thought that Mr Dick was a little out of his mind.

"Not a morsel," returned Miss Betsey. "If there is anything in the world that Mr Dick is not, it's that. He has been *called* mad," added Miss Betsey.

And after a little while she explained that he was a distant connection of hers, and that his near relations, imagining him mad, had put him into a private asylum, where he was not treated well; and that after a good deal of squabbling about it, Miss Betsey had got him out, and that Mr Dick had lived with her ever since.

"If he likes to fly a kite sometimes," said Miss Betsey, "what of that? Franklin used to fly a kite. He was a Quaker, or something of that sort, if I am not mistaken. And a Quaker flying a kite is a much more ridiculous object than anybody else."

Her generous championship of poor Mr Dick not only inspired hope in David's young breast; his heart warmed to Miss Betsey herself. He felt that though she was a rather eccentric old lady, she was to be trusted in and honoured.

He waited anxiously for Mr Murdstone's reply to Miss Betsey, and made himself as agreeable as he could to his aunt and Mr Dick; and would have gone out with the latter to fly the great kite, but that he had no other clothes than those belonging to Mr Dick, which confined him to the house.

At last the reply from Mr Murdstone came, and Miss Betsey informed him, to his terror, that Mr Murdstone was coming to speak to her himself the next day.

Sitting bundled up in Mr Dick's clothes next day, flushed and heated and anxious, he waited to see the harsh, gloomy face of his dreaded stepfather.

Miss Betsey sat sewing in the window, looking more imperious than ever, when suddenly David heard her give the alarm, "Janet! Donkeys!"

And to his consternation and amazement David beheld Miss Murdstone on a side-saddle ride deliberately over the sacred piece of green, and stop in front of the house, looking about her.

"Go along with you!" cried Miss Betsey, shaking her fist at the window. "You have no business there. How dare you trespass? Go along! Oh, you boldfaced thing!"

David cried out that it was Miss Murdstone, and that the gentleman walking behind was Mr Murdstone.

"I don't care who it is!" cried Miss Betsey, shaking her head. "I won't be trespassed upon; I won't allow it. Go away! Janet, turn him round. Lead him off!"

Janet tried to pull the donkey round by the bridle. Mr Murdstone tried to lead him on; Miss Murdstone struck at Janet with a parasol; and several boys, who had come to see the engagement, shouted vigorously; while Miss Betsey suddenly espying the donkey-boy, who was an old enemy of hers, rushed out on the scene of action, pounced on him, and dragged him, with his jacket over his head, into the garden, calling upon Janet to fetch the constables that he might be taken on the spot; but the donkey-boy soon dodged out of Miss Betsey's grasp, and went whooping away, taking his donkey with him, for Miss Murdstone had dismounted while Miss Betsey held the boy, and she now stood waiting with her brother at the bottom of the steps, until Miss Betsey should be at leisure to receive them.

Miss Trotwood, a little ruffled by the combat,

marched past them into the house with great dignity, and took no notice of their presence, until they were announced by Janet.

"Shall I go away, Aunt?" said David, trembling.

"No, sir," said Miss Betsey. "Certainly not." And she pushed him into a corner, and fenced him up with a chair; and Mr and Miss Murdstone entered the room.

"Oh!" said Miss Betsey, "I was not aware at first to whom I had the pleasure of objecting. But I don't allow anybody to ride over that turf."

"Your regulation is rather awkward to strangers," said Miss Murdstone.

"Is it?" said Miss Betsey.

"Miss Trotwood?" interposed Mr Murdstone.

"I beg your pardon," said Miss Betsey, giving him a keen look. "You are the Mr Murdstone who married the widow of my late nephew, David Copperfield."

"I am," said Mr Murdstone.

"You'll excuse my saying, sir," returned Miss Betsey, "that I think it would have been a much better and happier thing if you had left the poor child alone."

"I so far agree with what Miss Trotwood has remarked," said Miss Murdstone, "that I consider our lamented Clara to have been in all essential respects a mere child."

"It is a comfort to you and to me, ma'am," returned Miss Betsey, "who are getting on in life, and are not likely to be made unhappy by our personal attractions, that nobody can say the same of us!"

"No doubt," said Miss Murdstone, not with a very ready assent; while Miss Trotwood rang the bell, and told Janet to give her compliments to Mr Dick and beg him to come down.

Miss Betsey sat up very stiff, frowning at the wall until Mr Dick came in, biting his forefinger, and looking rather foolish.

"Mr Dick," said Miss Betsey, introducing him. "An old and intimate friend, on whose judgment I rely."

Mr Dick took his finger out of his mouth, and stood among the group with a very grave face.

"Miss Trotwood," said Mr Murdstone, "on the receipt of your letter, I considered it an act of greater justice to myself to answer it in person, rather than by letter. This unhappy boy, who has run away from his friends and his occupation, has been the occasion of much domestic trouble, both during the lifetime of my late dear wife, and since. He has a sullen, rebellious spirit, a violent temper, an untractable disposition. And I have felt that it is right you should, receive this grave announcement from our lips."

"And I beg to observe," added Miss Murdstone, "that of all the boys in the world, I believe this is the worst boy."

"Strong!" said Miss Betsey shortly. "Well, sir?" she questioned of Mr Murdstone.

Mr Murdstone, with his face darkening more and

more, explained that he had placed the boy "under the eye of a friend, in a respectable business."

"About the respectable business," said Miss Betsey, catching him up sharply, "if he had been your own boy you would have put him to it, just the same, I suppose?"

"If he had been my brother's own boy," returned Miss Murdstone striking in, "his character would have been altogether different."

After that Miss Betsey questioned Mr Murdstone very sharply about the house and garden at Blunderstone, asking how it was that the property had not been settled on the boy.

"My late wife loved her second husband, ma'am," said Mr Murdstone, "and trusted implicitly in him."

"Your late wife, sir, was a most unworldly, most unhappy, most unfortunate baby," returned Miss Trotwood, shaking her head at him. "That's what *she* was. And now what have you got to say next?"

"Merely this, Miss Trotwood. I am here to take David back; to take him back unconditionally, to dispose of him as I think proper, and to deal with him as I think right."

"And what does the boy say?" said Miss Betsey. "Are you ready to go, David?"

David cried out "No," and entreated her not to let him go, crying out that the Murdstones had never liked him; that they had made his mother, who always loved him dearly, unhappy about him; that he knew that well, and Peggotty knew it well. And he begged and prayed his aunt to befriend and protect him for his father's sake.

"Mr Dick," said Miss Betsey, "what shall I do with this child?"

"Have him measured for a suit of clothes directly," answered Mr Dick.

"Mr Dick," said Miss Betsey triumphantly, "give me your hand, for your common-sense is invaluable."

Shaking it cordially, she pulled David to her, and said to Mr Murdstone:

"You can go when you like; I'll take my chance with the boy. If he's all that you say he is, at least I can do as much for him then as you have done. But I don't believe a word of it."

"Miss Trotwood," said Mr Murdstone as he rose, "if you were a gentleman—"

"Bah! Stuff and nonsense!" said Miss Betsey. "Don't talk to me! Do you think I don't know what a woeful day it was for that soft little creature when you first came in her way—smirking and making great eyes at her as if you couldn't say boh! to a goose? Oh, yes, bless us! Who so smooth and silky as Mr Murdstone at first! The poor innocent had never seen such a man. He was made of sweetness. He worshipped her. He doted on her boy—tenderly doted on him! He was to be another father to him, and they were all to live together in a garden of roses, weren't they! Ugh! Get along with you, do!" said Miss Betsey.

"I never heard anything like this person in my life," said Miss Murdstone.

"Mr Murdstone," went on Miss Betsey, shaking her finger at him, and taking no notice whatever of Miss Murdstone, "you were a tyrant to the simple baby, and you broke her heart. . . . Ay, ay! you needn't wince. I know it's true without that."

Mr Murdstone had stood by the door, observing her all this while, with a smile upon his face. Now, though the smile was still in place, his black eyebrows were heavily contracted, and the colour had left his face, and he seemed to breathe as if he had been running.

"Good day, sir," said Miss Trotwood, "and good-bye! Good day to you too, ma'am," added Miss Betsey, turning suddenly on Miss Murdstone. "Let me see you ride a donkey over *my* green again, and as sure as you have a head upon your shoulders, I'll knock your bonnet off, and tread upon it!"

It was said in such a fiery way that Miss Murdstone, without a word, put her arm through her brother's, and walked haughtily out of the cottage. Miss Betsey remained in the window looking out after them; prepared, no doubt, in the case of the donkey's reappearance, to carry her threat into instant execution.

No attempt at defiance being made, however, her stern face gradually relaxed, and became so pleasant that David was emboldened to clasp his arms around her neck and kiss and thank her over and over again for her protection. He then shook hands with Mr

Dick, who shook hands with him a number of times, who hailed this happy close of the proceedings with repeated bursts of hearty laughter.

"You'll consider yourself guardian, jointly with me, of this child, Mr Dick," said Miss Trotwood.

"I shall be delighted," said Mr Dick, "to be the guardian of David's son."

"Very good," returned Miss Betsey, "*that's* settled. I have been thinking, do you know, Mr Dick, that I might call him Trotwood."

"Certainly, certainly. Call him Trotwood, certainly," said Mr Dick. "David's son Trotwood."

"Trotwood Copperfield, you mean," returned Miss Betsey.

"Yes, to be sure. Yes. Trotwood Copperfield," said Mr Dick.

Miss Betsey took so kindly to the notion that some ready-made clothes which were purchased for David that very afternoon were marked in her own handwriting, in indelible ink, "Trotwood Copperfield."

So he began his new life, in a new name, and with everything new about him, in a new and happy home, and here, I think, we must leave him in the good company of his staunch friends Miss Betsey and Mr Dick.

In time he came to put the memory of his Blunderstone life behind him and the remembrance of it became a hazy and distant one. Miss Betsey sent him to a good school to resume his education and he was delighted to be able to visit his dear friends

Peggotty and Barkis. He also met his comrades from happier times at Salem House, Steerforth and Traddles, again. The story of David Copperfield does not end here, however, as there were many other adventures embarked upon and adversities to be overcome on our young hero's journey to become a distinguished gentleman.